AGATHA WINNER

Red Card was the 2003 recipient of the prestigious Agatha Award for Best Children's /Young Adult Mystery.

The Agatha Awards honor traditional mysteries—books best typified by the works of Agatha Christie. The genre is loosely defined as mysteries that contain no gratuitous violence; usually featuring an amateur detective, a confined setting and characters who know one another.

Agatha contestants are nominated by the registered fans and Friends of Malice Domestic at their annual convention in Arlington, Virginia. Winners were selected by all attendees and presented at the Agatha Awards Banquet.

Fiftee~ ~~~~ ~~ ~~~ ~~~~ ~~~~~~~ ~~ tthew
LaBr **FAYETTEVILLE PUBLIC LIBRARY** n the
histoₗ **401 W MOUNTAIN ST.**
FAYETTEVILLE, AR 72701

RED CARD

For Don E. Hale, Pauline Hale, and
Donald and Mary LaBrot

Acknowledgments

Many thanks to Suzanne, Brent, Kate, and Tim, wonderful writers who gave us much-needed advice and support; Kathy, Gale, and Britt, for keeping the "fun" in dysfunctional while poring over the pages; Aaron, another fine writer who gave us great input; Martin and Laurie, for the painless shots; and last but certainly not least to Lisa at Top Publications, who believed in Zeke.

Red Card

by

Daniel J. Hale
&
Matthew LaBrot

Top Publications, Ltd.
Dallas, Texas

Red Card

A Top Publications Paperback
Second Printing, October 2003
12221 Merit Drive, Suite 750
Dallas, Texas 75251
ALL RIGHTS RESERVED
Copyright 2002
Daniel J. Hale
ISBN#: 1-929976-15-1
Library of Congress # 2002103207

Printed in the United States of America

Chapter One

Houston was so hot and muggy, it felt like I was playing soccer in an Amazon rainforest. The final seconds of the Dallas Sundogs' third game in the Lone Star Invitational were ticking off the clock. We were tied 3-3. The New Orleans Buccaneers had the ball, and they were moving it to the goal. If New Orleans scored, we'd be eliminated from the tournament.

Just as one of the Buccaneer forwards was lining up for a shot on goal, Rocky Whitehead stole the ball and left him behind in a cloud of dust. Rocky was one of the best sweepers in the league, something he'd just proven again. He ran up the side of the field, his light-blond hair glaring white in the sun.

Now was our chance. The Sundogs had to score on this drive. Otherwise, the game would go into overtime. Dallas may have been hot, but Houston was even hotter – like New Orleans. The Buccaneers were used to the heat and humidity, and a lot better prepared for extended play.

As Rocky got ready to pass the ball to Charlie Baldwin, several of the Buccaneers and even a few members of my own team started laughing and running in different directions. The referee blew his whistle. I thought the game was over until I looked down and saw the fast little animal with the furry tail scurrying across the field. *Oh, no!*

The squirrel darted first toward Rocky Whitehead, then Pow Wow Gao, then one of the Buccaneer forwards. All at once, he made a mad dash for the parents on the sidelines. Before Mrs. Gao could move, he'd scurried up her pants leg. She screamed so loud, you almost could have heard her back in Dallas. That must have scared the squirrel, because he quickly turned and hurried back down to the ground.

While the furry little rodent scampered off toward the tall pines near the Lone Star Soccer Park's parking lot, I noticed Mrs. Gao and several of the other parents staring at me. My teammates were giving me suspicious glances as well. Our coach, Ryan O'Connor, shook his head and smiled at the ground. I knew they suspected me of being responsible for the rampant squirrel.

They were right.

My name is Zeke Armstrong. I'm thirteen years old. I've got a secret. I also have a cowlick that won't go away. My hair and my eyes are brown. I was born in a treehouse in the jungle in Africa – just like Tarzan. Before I came to the United States to stay with Uncle Dane, I'd lived in seven different countries. My uncle said I had a real knack for finding trouble. He was right about that – I'd stumbled across some pretty serious situations in just about every place I ever lived. Even so, I'd been in Texas for almost a year, and the worst thing that had happened so far was that a few of my pranks didn't work out the way I'd planned. Like today.

How had that squirrel gotten out of his box? I hadn't planned to release him until after the game's final whistle. Even using the tricks I'd learned from the tribesmen in New Guinea, trapping that squirrel had taken over an hour. Now he'd escaped across the field and up the side of a pine tree in a matter of seconds.

If the referee thought the squirrel had been my doing, he didn't mention it. He just blew his whistle.

Moments after play resumed, Rocky Whitehead again had the ball. The game was suddenly as fast and furious as it'd been before. Rocky rushed up the side of the field. Coach

Ryan grabbed a handful of his own short red hair and shouted something from the sidelines. I was too far away to hear. Rocky darted past one of the Buccaneers, then passed the ball to Charlie Baldwin. All at once, there were three guys on Charlie. There was no way around them. Charlie's shaved head swiveled left and right, then he tipped the ball off of his heel and back to Pow Wow Gao.

Pow Wow may have been the smallest guy on our team, but he was also the fastest. He zigzagged through a line of Buccaneers, then ran toward an empty space that Charlie had just opened up. I expected Pow Wow to pass the ball back to Charlie, but when he was a few feet away, he dodged left and took the ball around the side. From the look on Charlie's face, Pow Wow's move surprised him. It also seemed to confuse the two Buccaneers who suddenly appeared on either side of Charlie. Pow and wow!

Pow Wow's real first name was Richard, but when he joined the team, he'd explained that "Gao" rhymed with "Pow" and "Wow". The nickname stuck. The first time I met him, I'd tried saying hello in Cantonese, then in Mandarin. He just looked at me like I was speaking Swahili. Pow Wow was the first Chinese kid I'd ever met who didn't understand

Chinese.

Coach Ryan yelled something else I couldn't hear. Pow Wow turned again and started moving the ball up the center of the field. He was heading straight for me. I knew what to do.

Using my best fake, I broke away from the freckle-faced Buccaneer defending me and got ready to take possession of the ball. Just then, I noticed Ian Crow, our other forward, cutting across the field. He'd left the stocky Buccaneer defender behind in a cloud of dust. Ian's long black hair flew wild as he moved into position.

Pow Wow Gao had three guys on his tail. He glanced at me, then at Ian. His eyes darted from side to side. He looked like an impala escaping a hungry pride of lions.

I wanted to score again, but Ian Crow was our best player. He was a better forward than me, and I knew he could make the shot. Besides, Ian's father was on the sidelines, chain-smoking cigarettes and shouting orders at Ian, like he always did. Mr. Crow had a bad temper. He kept telling Ian that if he didn't get more aggressive, he'd never play soccer for Stanford University. Ian had mentioned a couple of times that he wanted to go to Stanford, but it still seemed to mean more to his father than it did to him. I knew that if Ian didn't get a goal, Mr. Crow would probably get really angry – again.

Coach Ryan shouted something else I couldn't hear. Pow Wow kicked the ball to Rocky, who immediately crossed it to Ian. Now was Ian's chance. He started rushing the goal. Between him and the net, there was only one guy: the stocky kid who looked like he was the slowest of the Buccaneers.

Uncle Dane says things aren't always what they seem. He's always telling me a lot of stuff like that. As much as I hate to admit it, he's usually right. Once again, I came face to face with what he meant. The stocky Buccaneer defender suddenly poured on more speed than I thought a guy his size could manage. A moment later, he was blocking Ian's shot on the goal.

Coach Ryan shouted so loud that even I could hear. "Give it to Zeke!"

Ian didn't hesitate. He kicked the ball to the side, and it came blistering across the field toward me. There was no time to think, much less try anything fancy. I put up a shot on my first touch.

The ball sailed past the freckle-faced Buccaneer

defending me.

It went right between the Buccaneer goalie's legs.

The ball hit the back of the net.

Coach Ryan jumped up and down on the far sidelines and shouted, "Armstrong! Yes!" He looked more like a little kid than a twenty-five-year-old man. Coach Ryan was the kind of guy who got excited when things went well. He was also the kind of guy who got excited when things didn't go well. My teammates on the field started yelling and rushing toward me. On the near sidelines, the team parents shouted and waved Sundogs banners and rang cowbells. It was so loud, I could barely hear the referee blowing his whistle.

Coach Ryan, my teammates, and the Sundogs parents suddenly got quiet.

The ref made his call. "Offsides!"

I stood there, not understanding. The freckle-faced Buccaneer had been upfield from me when I took my shot on goal. It went right past him when I kicked it into the net. I was sure of it. I wondered if that was the referee's way of getting even with me for the squirrel incident.

It didn't make any difference. The ref had made his call. We were going into overtime – without Coach Ryan.

Chapter Two

There were a couple of times at tournaments in the past when Coach Ryan would, as he explained it, "strongly emphasize his point." He'd gotten a yellow card that way once a few months ago. This afternoon, though, the referee must have thought he was emphasizing his point *too* strongly. He red-carded our coach.

I couldn't believe it.

First the ref called my shot offside, then he forced Coach Ryan off the field.

Uncle Dane would say that we had to respect the referee's decisions – even when he made bad calls and gave our coach a red card. If Mom and Dad were there, they'd be joining the rest of the Sundogs parents on the sidelines shouting, "Rip-off! Rip-off!"

Coach Ryan's face turned almost as red as his hair as he headed across the field. I'd never seen him that angry. He spoke a few words to Ian Crow's father, who was standing there with a man in a black hat, a man I'd never seen before. Coach Ryan stormed off toward the parking lot.

When Ian's dad joined the Sundogs on our side of the field, I could tell that he was angry, too. Mr. Crow crushed one cigarette on the ground, lit another, then started barking orders at us. He even swore a couple of times. Ian's dad had played soccer for a small college back East, and he'd spent some time on a professional team in France as well. This was a good thing. The New Orleans Buccaneers would be stiff competition in overtime – we needed a strong coach. Right before we took the field, though, Mr. Crow apologized for his "use of strong language." He said he wasn't angry with us, though he didn't say with whom he *was* upset.

Chapter Three

Overtime was fierce. One of the Buccaneers shoved Ian Crow to the ground just as Ian was getting ready to kick the ball into the net. The referee didn't even call a penalty on New Orleans. Mr. Crow was furious, but he didn't say a word. I took a knee alongside Ian while Mr. Crow checked him over. Ian said he felt funny, like he could barely breathe. Mr. Crow pulled his son from the game and substituted Charlie Baldwin as forward.

It was Charlie who kicked in the winning goal.

When the game was over, the man in the black hat left the field. Everyone else – parents and players alike – ran over to rub Charlie Baldwin's shaved head. Charlie's dad even managed to hobble across the field on his cane to congratulate his son. I hadn't seen Mr. Baldwin that happy since before he'd had that bad wreck a few months ago. Everyone seemed proud of Charlie. Everyone except Ian Crow's dad, that is.

Mr. Crow walked over and spoke to Ian. I was

standing close enough to hear what he said. His voice sounded angry. He said something about Coach Ryan trying to "thwart the career of a gifted player." Mr. Crow lit another cigarette and walked away. Ian just stood there, looking down at the ground.

As I started wondering what Mr. Crow meant, I heard some of the other boys laughing. I looked over to see Rocky Whitehead standing in the middle of a group of Sundogs. His face was beet-red compared to his light-blond hair. Some of my teammates were pointing and snickering and saying, "Soft on the inside!"

I got a little closer to see that Rocky was holding a small box of Creamy Puffs cereal – the one I'd hidden in his team bag as a gag. I'd meant for him to pull it out after he got back to his room. It never occurred to me that he'd find it there on the field. Poor Rocky. He was humiliated, and I felt bad. Practical jokes weren't funny when people got hurt. Today was definitely not a good day for pranks.

Chapter Four

I tried lying on my side.

I tried scrunching up my pillow.

I tried counting sheep, but I'd never seen a real sheep.

I tried counting antelope instead.

That didn't work either.

It was no use. I'd never get back to sleep. It was already daylight outside, and I was as jumpy as a cat. The motel air conditioner rattled and hissed so loudly, it reminded me of that rickety old bus careening down the steep mountain road in the Andes. Just thinking about it made me tense. Not only that, but Ian Crow was tossing and turning in the other bed.

As long as I'd known Ian, he'd been a worrier. It just surprised me that he could actually worry in his sleep. Right now, I wondered if he was dreaming that something bad had happened to Coach Ryan.

The coach hadn't come to the team dinner last night, and he didn't even make it back for lights-out. I figured he'd gone away somewhere to be alone and think. When Coach Ryan had gotten that yellow card a few months ago in Dallas, he'd gone to his office at Whitehead Medical Supply so he could be alone and "ponder his actions." Rocky Whitehead's dad's company was a big one, and they even had a warehouse in Houston. I wondered if maybe the coach had gone there to think by himself.

I was concerned about Coach Ryan, but it never occurred to me that he wouldn't be there for the game with the Miami Hurricanes this morning. That game was the main thing making me edgy.

In a situation like this, Uncle Dane would probably say, "At least there *is* a next game, Zeke." I guess he'd be right. If we'd lost to New Orleans yesterday afternoon, we wouldn't be facing Miami today. Still, though, I was nervous.

I looked at the clock on the nightstand. It was 6:05 in the morning. In ten minutes, the alarm would go off. A few hours from now, the Sundogs would go up against the Hurricanes. The winner of that game would advance to the quarter-finals in the Lone Star Invitational. Last year, Miami had knocked the Sundogs out of the tournament. I wasn't with the Sundogs then – I was still living with my parents in Peru – but the guys told me that the Hurricanes were brutal.

All the other guys were probably just as tense about this morning's game as I was. The Sundogs and the team parents had a meeting on the field at 6:45. The way I had it figured, that meeting was going to turn into one big, long worry-fest. What we Sundogs needed was something to take our minds off of our troubles. For that, there was nothing quite like a good practical joke.

It was a twenty-minute drive from the motel to the playing fields' parking lot. Many of the parents liked to get there early. That meant they'd be leaving soon. If I was going to slip out and set up everything, I had to act fast.

I got out of bed and quietly made my way through the mounds of clothes strewn everywhere. Ian Crow was a nice guy and the best player on our team, but he was also a real slob. I pulled a clean soccer uniform from the chest-of-drawers, then hurried into the bathroom to change clothes and wash my face. When I looked in the mirror, I noticed that my hair was sticking up in back. As usual. I wet a comb and tried my best to flatten the cowlick. It didn't help. I wondered if it would help if I grew my hair long like Ian's, or if I had it all shaved off like Charlie Baldwin and his dad did. Neither choice seemed right for me, though.

It took a couple of minutes before I found my sports watch buried under a pile of Ian's clothes. As I strapped it on my wrist, I noticed a copy of *Ezekial Tobias and the Lost Inca Gold* lying on a chair nearby. The illustration on the cover was of a colorfully painted bus heading down a treacherous mountain road. I got goose bumps just looking at the picture. Of all the things Ian could have brought with him to read, why did he have to pick that book?

I stuffed a clean towel, fresh socks, shin guards, and shoes into my team bag, then tossed in my trusty fake knife and the packets of stage blood that Uncle Dane's last girlfriend had given me. I thought about what a mess the fake blood would make, so I added another towel to my bag. Finally, I grabbed the mobile phone Uncle Dane asked me to keep with me from the charger and clipped it to the waistband of my shorts. I was ready to go.

As quickly and quietly as I could, I opened the door and walked out. When I shut the door behind me, I heard Ian's alarm clock go off with a loud buzz. It was warm and humid outside, but much cooler than it had been yesterday afternoon. I liked early morning. In places like Houston – and Kinshasa and Quito and Jakarta – it was the best part of the day. Not too hot.

I hurried barefoot along the second-floor walkway and started down the stairs. In the parking lot below, the tops of the cars were wet with dew. All the cars except Dr. Gao's sleek black Corvette convertible, that is – he always kept it covered with a blue canvas tarp. My dad taught me to drive on the Serengeti Plains when I was seven years old. Since then, I'd gotten to drive a lot of different types of vehicles, including that rickety old bus, but I'd never been behind the wheel of a car like Dr. Gao's Corvette. I would have given almost anything to take it out for a spin.

When I reached the bottom step, a loud, sharp sound rang out. It sounded like a gunshot, but I figured it was probably just a car backfiring somewhere in the distance. After all, this was Houston, Texas, not some war-torn Third World country. I sat down and quickly began to pull on my shin guards, socks, and shoes. A vehicle started up somewhere nearby. It sounded like a gasoline-powered pickup or SUV, maybe even a minivan. I glanced out at the parking lot, but all the cars and trucks and vans appeared to be empty. A moment later, the engine revved. I looked around again. There were no lights, there was no motion in the parking lot or out on the highway. The vehicle roared away, and its sound quickly faded into the distance. I saw nothing.

That's strange, I thought. I glanced at my sports watch. It was 6:18.

Once I'd laced up my shoes, I hurried around the corner of the building and looked up to see that the red neon sign read "No Vacancy." The Sundogs and the team parents had rented every room in the small motel. Since Uncle Dane was in Europe on a book-signing tour, I'd gone to the tournament with the Gaos. On the drive from Dallas to Houston, Pow Wow's mom had said that all the motels and hotels within thirty miles of the playing field area were completely booked. The Lone Star Invitational was one of the largest and most important soccer tournaments in the country. I wished my parents could be there to see me play.

Dad's a doctor, and Mom's an architect. They work for an international relief organization. Their job is to build hospitals and clinics in remote areas with poor medical care.

Ever since I was born in that treehouse, we never stayed anywhere longer than two years. When it was time for me to start junior high school, my folks moved to India and I came to live with my uncle in Dallas. I like Uncle Dane a lot, but I miss my parents.

As I passed the motel office, I looked in through the picture window to see a burly man standing behind the counter. He was reading a newspaper. He noticed me walking by as he took a sip from the steaming white Styrofoam cup in his hand. I waved. He smiled, put down his coffee, and waved back.

A big white van with two long ladders strapped to the top pulled in behind me. The headlights went off, and a Hispanic man stepped out. The sign on the van's door read "Escondido Building Contractors." The burly man from the motel office walked out, shook the Hispanic man's hand, then pointed at something above the picture window.

Juggling my ball from knee to knee, I approached the high wooden fence that stood between the motel and the soccer fields. Because some of the roads in this part of Houston had been closed for construction, it was a twenty-minute drive from the motel to the playing field area parking lot. It only took a few seconds – and a lot of agility – to jump the fence. Pow Wow Gao, Ian Crow, and I had found this shortcut yesterday morning.

I kicked the ball over. When it landed on the other side, I heard a muffled thud. It wasn't the sound a ball hitting grass should have made. *That's funny.* I slipped the shoulder strap of my team bag over my head, then ran at the fence and jumped. I caught the tops of a couple of the rough wooden planks with my fingertips then, feet scrambling, pulled myself up.

Twenty-four soccer fields lay spread out before me like an immense green lawn – a lawn with forty-eight regulation goals. When I looked down, I saw my soccer ball lying there on the grass. A red stain covered one of the white patches. I couldn't figure out how it'd gotten there. I pulled myself up further and got ready to drop my team bag.

When I looked down, I saw something I didn't expect to see. A red-haired man lay beside the fence. His eyes were closed. His face was pale. He was still wearing the clothes he'd had on yesterday afternoon. For a moment, I thought he might be sleeping. Then I noticed the bloody patch on his forehead. I knew he must be unconscious. Or worse.

My heart started beating fast. I pitched down my team bag then cleared the top of the fence and landed next to Coach Ryan. Blood was flowing from his head wound. I remembered the loud bang I'd heard. The coach had been shot!

I knelt beside Coach Ryan and put my face close to his. He was breathing, but only barely. I could smell smoke in his clothes and in his hair. It was not the smoke from a campfire or a fireplace, and it wasn't the smoke from a cigarette. He smelled like those men in the Caribbean who play checkers in the park while they puff on big cigars.

While I called out, "Help! Help!" I reached into my bag, pitched my fake knife and the stage blood packets onto the grass, then pulled out a clean towel. With one hand, I pressed the towel to the wound to stop the bleeding. With the other, I grabbed my mobile phone and dialed 9-1-1.

Chapter Five

The motel manager and Señor Escondido, the Hispanic man who'd been driving the white van, heard me call for help. They tried to climb over the fence, but it was too tall. I shouted for the manager to go get Dr. Gao. While the 9-1-1 operator kept me on the line, Señor Escondido found a weak spot several yards away and removed some of the planks. Coach Ryan stopped breathing. My dad had taught me CPR, and I'd once used it to save a man's life: the American Ambassador to Indonesia had had a heart attack while I was mountain-biking with him and his son. I was going to try to save Coach Ryan's life the same way, but then Dr. Gao rushed through the new hole in the fence. I moved aside and let him do his job. As he worked to save Coach Ryan's life, parents and players began to stream through the gap.

Three police squad cars and an ambulance arrived

within minutes. The police officers moved back the parents and the players. They then roped off the area with yellow crime scene tape strung up on metal posts they'd driven into the ground. A couple of uniformed officers guarded the gap in the tall fence separating the motel from the soccer fields. Two emergency medical technicians strapped Coach Ryan to a stretcher and hurried him across the crime scene area. A policeman unhooked the yellow tape from the top of one of the thin metal posts and lowered it to the ground as EMTs approached with Coach Ryan. He replaced it after they passed. The EMTs put the stretcher in the back of the ambulance, and Dr. Gao got in with the coach. The ambulance sped away with its siren blaring and the lights on top flashing.

I glanced at my watch. It was 6:38. Only twenty minutes had passed since the shot rang out while I was lacing my shoes. Someone in the vehicle I heard start up and race away had probably fired that shot. I wondered who it could have been, and why he or she would want to hurt Coach Ryan.

The coach was a nice guy. Uncle Dane said he was "a fine human being – a real mensch." I didn't know exactly what a "mensch" was, but I knew enough to know that it was a compliment. Even the coach's ex-girlfriend still liked him, and that was really saying something. None of the women Uncle Dane had dated in the past would speak to him anymore. Coach Ryan didn't have any enemies that anyone knew of. Why, then, would someone want to kill him?

Whatever the reason, I knew that whoever had done it wasn't standing there with us. As I looked around and tried to figure out who wasn't there, a big white car drove out onto the field and stopped nearby. A pretty, dark-haired lady in a tan suit got out, then walked over and talked to one of the uniformed officers. He handed her something, then pointed at me.

The lady came over and said, "You must be Zeke. I'm Detective García."

I shook her hand and said, "I'm the one who found him."

"So I hear." She smiled. "Where did you learn CPR?"

"My dad's a doctor."

The detective held up a couple of plastic bags. In them were my fake knife and the packets of stage blood. She asked, "These belong to you?"

My face felt hot. "I was going to play a little joke on the guys and the parents."

"I see…" Her voice trailed off, then she pulled a notepad from her pocket. "I want you to tell me everything you can think of, starting from the beginning."

Sweat trickled down my back as I told her exactly what I'd seen, heard, and smelled. I then said, "Whoever did it isn't here."

She stopped writing, looked up at me and asked, "Why do you say that, Zeke?"

I pointed at my watch. "It's a twenty-minute drive from the soccer field to the motel." I pointed at the hole in the fence. "Those police officers haven't let anyone in or out since they got here, and that was about twelve minutes after I heard the SUV or pickup or whatever it was start up and drive away. Whoever shot Coach Ryan must have been in that vehicle. He or she didn't have time to make it back to the motel."

Detective García gave me a smile that made me wonder if she was taking me seriously.

"Really, I know what I'm talking about." As the detective closed her notebook, I added, "This isn't the first time I've helped to solve a crime."

Detective García smiled again, thanked me for helping with their investigation then handed me a business card with her name and phone number on it. When she walked away – still holding my fake knife and blood – to join the uniformed officers in the crime scene area, I looked down and shook my head. I probably shouldn't have mentioned the other crimes I'd helped to solve. The detective probably thought I was just some stupid kid trying to impress her.

Even if she didn't take me seriously, though, I knew I was right. I looked around the crowd. My teammates were all there, as were the team moms. Dr. Gao was with Coach Ryan. Other than him, three of the team fathers were missing. Those three were Charlie Baldwin's dad, Ian Crow's dad, and Rocky Whitehead's dad.

Uncle Dane told me that most crimes are committed by people who know their victim. Random acts of violence were pretty rare. It was hard to imagine, but it appeared that Mr. Baldwin, Mr. Crow, or Mr. Whitehead might have shot Coach Ryan. But why?

Chapter Six

The police talked to everyone on the field. When the last of the Sundog parents had been interviewed, Detective García spoke to Pow Wow Gao's mom for a few minutes. Then the detective got back in her big white car and drove away.

Mrs. Gao shouted, "Sundogs! Meeting in five minutes in the motel parking lot." For such a small woman, she had a very loud voice. Pow Wow's mom was good at handling people, schedules, and money, too. It was no wonder that we'd made her the team manager.

Everyone filed past the two uniformed police officers guarding the hole in the fence. Hardly anyone said a word. When the last of us passed through, I heard one of the officers ask Señor Escondido to replace the missing planks.

The Sundogs and the parents gathered in the motel parking lot at the base of the stairs. Pow Wow Gao, Charlie Baldwin and Ian Crow stood around me. Rocky Whitehead was standing off to the side by himself. He'd been acting extra tough since finding that cereal box in his team bag yesterday afternoon. I still felt pretty bad about that.

Mrs. Gao climbed a couple of steps and said, "Sundogs, I think it would be a good idea for us to use the buddy system from now on. If you're going outside, take a buddy with you. Okay?"

There was a low murmur that ran through the crowd, but no one – not even any of the parents – disagreed.

Mrs. Gao cleared her throat and continued, "We're all going to caravan over to the hospital in just a few minutes. Before we leave, though, we have an important decision to make." She paused and looked around at the members of our group.

Another low murmur passed through the crowd. From the expressions on their faces, no one seemed to know what she meant.

Mrs. Gao spoke again. "Are the Sundogs going to stay in the tournament, or are we going to drop out?"

It quickly became very noisy. One of the parents shouted, "Let's put it to a vote!"

Mrs. Gao called out, "Okay, everyone. Simmer

down."

The crowd fell silent.

She took a deep breath and said, "First, let's find out how many of those present want to stay in the tournament."

Some of the parents and players started shaking their heads and talking among themselves in low whispers. Even so, not a single hand was raised.

"Okay, those in favor of –" Mrs. Gao's purse started ringing. She fished her mobile phone out of her bag, flipped it open, and answered.

From the soft tone of her voice and the comforting words she spoke, I figured she was talking to some relative or friend of Coach Ryan. She told whoever it was that the Sundogs were dropping out of the tournament so that we could wait with the coach at the hospital. All at once, her tone changed. She then began to say, "Oh, I see," over and over again.

Mrs. Gao flipped her phone shut. Voice cracking, she looked at us and said, "That was Patrick O'Connor, Ryan's father. He and Mrs. O'Connor are on a flight from Dallas to Houston. They should reach the hospital in a little over an hour." Mrs. Gao looked like she was about to say something else, but then lowered her head as if she were trying not to cry. When she spoke again, though, her voice was strong and loud. "Mr. O'Connor said his son believed the Sundogs could win this tournament. Ryan wanted that more than anything. Mr. O'Connor told me that when Ryan wakes up, he'll be really upset if he finds out that we were even thinking about quitting." Mrs. Gao took a deep breath. "Well, what do you say, Sundogs? Are we in or are we out?"

As if we'd been trained to answer on cue, parents and players alike, we all shouted, "In!"

Mrs. Gao gave a smile that looked like it was hard for her to make. "Okay, then. We're staying in. There's only one thing we need – a coach."

That was one thing we *didn't* need to put to a vote. Ian Crow's father may have had a bad temper, and he always smelled like an ashtray, but he'd proven himself to be a good coach in overtime yesterday.

Mrs. Gao looked at Ian Crow and asked, "Ian, where's your dad?"

Ian shrugged then looked down. His hair fell over his eyes like a long black curtain. Mr. Crow was a pretty strict father, so it surprised me that he'd let Ian wear his hair that long. Ian's mother, Mrs. Jennings, was now married to a country-and-western singer. Ian lived with her most of the time. I figured she must have been the one who gave Ian permission to grow his hair.

Mrs. Gao looked around the crowd. "Has anyone seen Seth Crow?"

One of the team dads ran to Mr. Crow's room and knocked on the door, but no one answered. Two more dads announced that they were going to scout out the motel parking lot. They came back a few moments later and said that Mr. Crow's red pickup wasn't there. I glanced over at Ian to see that he was still looking down. Where was Ian's dad? He hadn't made it to the team dinner last night, but I figured it was because we ate in a non-smoking restaurant. I wondered if Mr. Crow could have been the one who…

No. It just didn't seem to fit.

Mrs. Gao glanced at her watch and announced, "It's 7:45. Our game against the Miami Hurricanes is at 10:30. If we can't find Mr. Crow by then, my husband will fill in as coach."

Pow Wow, Charlie and I looked at each other. No one said a word, but each of us knew what the others were thinking. *We're doomed.* Dr. Gao was a nice man, and we liked him a lot, but he didn't know how to coach a soccer team.

Mrs. Gao then announced, "Okay, everyone. Let's go to the hospital."

The crowd began to break up, and I had another look around. There was no sign of Mr. Crow, Mr. Whitehead, or Mr. Baldwin. As we made our way through the parking lot, I looked for Mr. Whitehead's gleaming white Ford Expedition, the new one he'd bought after his last SUV was stolen, and the old camper truck Mr. Baldwin had been driving. Neither of the vehicles were there.

Chapter Seven

On the way to the hospital, Mrs. Gao drove more like a race car driver in the Indy 500 than a soccer mom in a minivan. Pow Wow sat in the front passenger seat – he seemed relaxed, like he was used to his mom's driving. Ian Crow, Charlie Baldwin, and I rode in the back, holding on for dear life. The way Mrs. Gao zipped through the thick Houston traffic, I wondered if she thought she was behind the wheel of Dr. Gao's sleek black Corvette convertible.

Neither Ian nor Charlie nor I were surprised that we reached the hospital first. We walked into the emergency room entrance, and Mrs. Gao went to the front desk to ask about Coach Ryan. Pow Wow, Ian, Charlie, and I went over and stood by the vending machines in the far corner of the waiting room. I could tell that Ian, Pow Wow, and Charlie were anxious for news about the coach. I was concerned, too, but I knew that the doctors were busy trying to save Coach Ryan's life. It might take a long time before they had a chance to give us any word about his condition.

Dr. Gao appeared from behind a door marked "No Admittance". He spoke to his wife for a few moments, pushing his glasses higher on his nose several times. Mrs. Gao motioned for us to stay where we were, then they both walked through the "No Admittance" door.

The other players and parents began to fill the waiting room. Doing something Uncle Dane called "post-crime reconnaissance," I stood there and watched carefully. No one acted suspiciously. Rocky Whitehead and his pretty mom were the last ones of our group to walk in. Whitehead was a good name for them: Rocky and both of his parents had hair so blond that it was almost white. Mrs. Whitehead had been a model. When Rocky was four years old, he'd starred in a television commercial for Creamy Puffs cereal. In it, Rocky said that Creamy Puffs were crunchy on the outside and soft in the middle. The commercial was still aired on Saturday morning TV. Mr. Whitehead owned Whitehead Medical Supplies. When Coach Ryan wasn't coaching, he worked for Mr. Whitehead's company. Charlie Baldwin's dad used to work for Whitehead Medical Supply – before the accident.

I hadn't seen Rocky's dad since dinner last night. His

mobile phone had rung while we were eating dessert, then he left, never to return. Where had Mr. Whitehead gone? Where was he now?

For that matter, I wondered where Mr. Baldwin could be.

I asked Charlie Baldwin where his dad was, but he just shrugged and ran his hand across his shaved head like he was trying to rub something off of it. Neither Charlie nor his dad had come to the team dinner last night, but that wasn't unusual. Since Mr. Baldwin had had his wreck, they never came to team dinners. Mr. Baldwin said the wreck left him in too much pain to work, so he quit his job at Whitehead Medical Supply and sued the driver of the other car. I'd overheard Dr. and Mrs. Gao saying that Mr. Baldwin had been arrested for drunk driving when he had the wreck, and that it appeared to them that he might be faking his injuries. None of that mattered a whole lot to me – I just felt bad for Charlie. He was a nice guy and a good soccer player.

Rocky Whitehead was leaning against the wall on the far side of the room, trying to look tough. Once the guys found out that Rocky had been in that television commercial, they started calling him "Creamy Puff" and telling him that he was soft in the middle. That was about the same time Rocky started pulling the tough-guy act. He was acting more tough than usual now, and that was my fault. I decided to wait a while before asking him where his father was.

Ian had been with me ever since I'd asked him about his dad back at the motel, so I knew better than to ask again. Ian was nervous enough as it was.

Several minutes passed before Dr. Gao and his wife walked out of the "No Admittance" door. Mrs. Gao's face was very pale. I'd seen that look on a lot of different faces in a lot of different countries. Even in the United States, I knew it was not a good sign.

Chapter Eight

The Gaos joined Pow Wow, Ian, Charlie, and me in the far corner of the waiting room. When everyone gathered around, Dr. Gao spoke. "Fortunately, the bullet only grazed Ryan's head. The blow was quite serious, nonetheless. He's been stabilized, but it could be hours before he regains consciousness… if he does so at all."

Several of the team moms gasped.

Dr. Gao continued, "For the time being there's nothing else anyone can do for him."

One of the team dads whispered out loud. "We can pray."

Dr. Gao nodded. "The doctors will be moving Ryan from the emergency room to the intensive care unit in a few minutes." He glanced at his watch, then asked, "Any word from Mr. Crow?"

A few of the parents shook their heads. Ian Crow looked down, and his long hair covered his eyes.

Dr. Gao pushed his glasses higher on his nose and continued, "I'm going to stay here until the O'Connors arrive, then I'll join you on the field." He gave a smile that looked tired. "Meanwhile, it's time for the Dallas Sundogs to get ready to win one for Coach Ryan."

A middle-aged couple walked into the waiting room. Neither of them was very tall. They both had blue eyes and red hair and rosy cheeks. I knew they must be Coach Ryan's parents.

Dr. and Mrs. Gao hurried away to greet the couple. After they'd talked for a few moments, Dr. Gao led them off through the "No Admittance" door. Mrs. Gao came back and told us that the couple was, in fact, Mr. and Mrs. O'Connor. She said that Dr. Gao would stay there with them until shortly before game time.

There was still no sign of Ian Crow's dad. It was starting to look as if the Dallas Sundogs would go up against the Miami Hurricanes with Dr. Gao as our coach. No one said anything, but it was pretty obvious that my teammates were disappointed. Miami was one of the best teams in the tournament. Mr. Crow may have had a bad temper, and I didn't like the way he put pressure on Ian, but he was a good coach. Everyone knew it, including Pow Wow Gao's father. I was sure Dr. Gao hoped just as much as the rest of us that Mr. Crow would show up before the game.

When the team and the parents filed outside into the Houston heat, we saw an empty police car parked in the emergency room driveway. Pow Wow, Ian, Charlie, and I piled into the Gaos' minivan. As Mrs. Gao sped out of the parking lot, I looked through the side window to see two uniformed police officers putting a man into the back of the police car. The man was dressed in pale-green clothes, like the ones doctors wear in the operating room. He had one of those pale-green caps on, too. Just as I started wondering why the police were arresting a doctor, the man turned and I got a good look at his face.

It wasn't a doctor.

It was Ian Crow's dad.

Chapter Nine

When Ian Crow saw what was happening to his father, he opened the back door and tried to jump out of the minivan – while it was still moving. Pow Wow, Charlie, and I held him back. It was like wrestling a wild animal. Mrs. Gao did a U-turn and wheeled back into the lot. One of the team fathers parked nearby jumped out of his car and helped us restrain Ian. A moment later, Dr. Gao hurried out of the emergency room entrance.

The police car sped out of the lot. Dr. Gao pulled Mrs. Gao aside, spoke to her for a few moments, then he had a word in private with Ian. Ian seemed to calm down a lot, then he and Dr. Gao got into the car with the team father parked nearby. The three of them drove away.

As we drove – slowly – back to the soccer fields, Mrs. Gao told Pow Wow, Charlie, and me what had happened. When Dr. Gao escorted the O'Connors into the ER to see Coach Ryan, there was a great hubbub in the hallway outside the coach's room. Two police officers were holding a man dressed in green operating room clothing and a surgical mask. One of the officers pulled off the mask. It was Mr. Crow. The nurse standing there told the officers that she walked into Coach Ryan's room and found Mr. Crow holding a pillow over the coach's face.

When Mrs. Gao finished talking, Charlie Baldwin asked, "Did the coach get hurt any worse?"

She replied, "It's too soon to tell."

Chapter Ten

By the time we reached the soccer field parking lot, everyone was talking about Mr. Crow's arrest. I couldn't figure out how everyone had heard about it so quickly, until I noticed one of the team fathers holding something that looked like a walkie-talkie. Uncle Dane had one of those. It was a police scanner. The word going around the crowd now was that Mr. Crow had been arrested for what happened in the emergency room, as well as for holding Coach Ryan hostage last night and shooting him this morning.

I couldn't explain why Ian's dad had disguised himself as a surgeon, and I didn't know why he'd been found holding a pillow over Coach Ryan's face, but I didn't believe that he'd shot the coach. For one thing, it wasn't Mr. Crow's pickup that I'd heard start up and race away while I was tying my shoelaces. Uncle Dane kept a truck just like it on his ranch up in Wyoming. The engine ran on diesel fuel. It made a loud, clattering sound when it started. The vehicle I'd heard this morning had a smoother, quieter, gasoline-powered engine. Another thing that caused me to doubt that Mr. Crow had held Coach Ryan hostage was the smoky odor in Coach Ryan's hair and on his clothes. What I'd smelled was cigar smoke, which was something like burning leather and sweet cherries. It was different from Mr. Crow's sour cigarette odor.

Uncle Dane had told me that my mobile phone was for emergencies only. This certainly seemed to me to be an emergency. I flipped open the phone, pulled Detective García's card from my team bag and dialed the number.

She answered on the second ring. "García."

"Hi." I cleared my throat. "This is Zeke Armstrong."

"Ah, yes. The boy who solves crimes." The detective chuckled. It didn't sound like a mean laugh, but it was a laugh just the same.

I swallowed the lump in my throat. "Actually, Detective García, that's why I called. You've got the wrong man. Mr. Crow didn't hold Coach Ryan hostage, and he didn't shoot him."

The detective laughed again. This time, it sounded less friendly than it had a few moments ago. "Zeke, I've heard from some of the other parents that you've got a bad reputation for pulling stunts like this. Frankly, I don't have time–"

"It's not a joke! Please listen."

The detective didn't say anything, so I continued. "For one thing, the SUV or pickup or whatever it was I heard this morning ran on gasoline. Mr. Crow's pickup has a diesel engine. For another thing, the smoke I smelled on Coach Ryan was cigar smoke. Mr. Crow smokes cigarettes, not cigars."

Detective García said nothing.

"You can check your notes. I told you all of this on the soccer field this morning."

There was silence on the other end of the line.

"Hello? Detective? Are you there?"

She didn't answer.

"Detective!"

"Yes, Zeke?" Detective García's voice was very calm.

I doubted that she'd heard anything I'd said. For a moment, I thought about just hanging up and trying to forget about the whole mess. I couldn't do that, though. Someone had shot Coach Ryan. Whoever did do it was still out there running around. So, once again, I ran through the details.

When I finished this time, the detective said, "Thank you for your input, Mr. Armstrong."

From the tone of her voice and the way she called me "Mr. Armstrong," I knew she was trying to get rid of me. It was no use to try to convince her. I thanked her and hung up.

If I was going to get the detective's attention, I had to figure out who *did* shoot the coach. I had to give Detective García a name. Whoever shot Coach Ryan probably knew he wasn't dead. Since the coach could wake up and tell the authorities who'd shot him, it would make sense for that person to keep out of sight. I looked around the crowd there on the field.

There were only two of the team fathers I couldn't account for. One was Charlie Baldwin's dad. The other was Mr. Whitehead. I hadn't seen either of them since yesterday afternoon and last night. The thing was, I'd never seen either of them smoking cigars.

Just then, a white Ford Expedition pulled up in the parking lot. It looked like Mr. Whitehead's SUV, but the windows were so darkly tinted that I couldn't tell who was inside. The last three letters on the license plate on the front bumper were "ETA" – my initials. The driver's door opened, and Mr. Whitehead stepped out. His shirt and pants – the same clothes he'd had on last night – were dirty. His thick blond hair was messed up, and it looked like he hadn't shaved since yesterday.

Mrs. Whitehead hurried over to her husband, and they talked for a few moments. I was too far away to hear anything they said, but it looked like she was angry and relieved at the same time. When he put his arm around her, she pulled away. It was then that I noticed a large bandage on the back of Mr. Whitehead's left hand. It hadn't been there at the team dinner last night. I knew this because I'd been sitting across the table from him. I wondered what Mr. Whitehead had done to it – and when and where. The Whiteheads exchanged a few more words that looked like an argument, then Mr. Whitehead got back into his Expedition, slammed the door, and stormed out of the parking lot.

As Mrs. Whitehead stood there, the Baldwins' old silver pickup with the camper shell on back pulled up in the parking lot. Mrs. Whitehead glanced over at the old camper truck then hurried back into the crowd, like she was trying to avoid someone. The driver's door squeaked open. Mr. Baldwin eased out of the truck and began hobbling along on his cane toward the other parents. All of his hair was cut off, just like his son's. Charlie had told me that his dad shaved both of their heads because haircuts were too expensive. I didn't know Mr. Baldwin very well before his accident, but, from what the other kids told me, it sounded like he'd been a pretty nice guy. Now he was always in a bad mood. Uncle Dane said that physical pain and money problems could "wreak havoc" on people's lives. I wondered if Mr. Baldwin's troubles had led him to shoot the coach.

Charlie's dad hadn't been at the team dinner last night. This was the first time I'd seen him since yesterday's game. I didn't know where he'd been all this time, but I intended to find out.

As I approached Mr. Baldwin, it suddenly occurred to me that I had no idea what I was going to say. When I was a couple of feet away, Mr. Baldwin stopped short and asked, "What do you want?"

Not knowing what else to say, I blurted out, "I was wondering if you'd heard about Mr. Crow."

"Your roommate's daddy?" Mr. Baldwin gave a smile that didn't seem happy at all. "They're going to lock him up and throw away the key for killing Ryan O'Connor."

It felt like someone punched me in the stomach. "Coach Ryan is dead?"

Mr. Baldwin's eyebrows arched. "You hadn't heard?"

I shook my head.

He gave another smile that wasn't really a smile. "Sorry to be the bearer of such bad news."

I stood there, staring. How could Coach Ryan be dead? How could such a nice guy as Charlie Baldwin have such a mean father? I turned and walked back into the crowd.

As I stood there, wondering how Pow Wow, Rocky, and the rest of my teammates were going to take the news, I noticed Mr. Baldwin talking to some of the other parents. He was no longer smiling a smile that wasn't really a smile. In fact, he looked very unhappy. A few moments later, Mr. Baldwin walked away from the group. He grabbed his son by the arm – hard, from the way Charlie winced – and spoke a few words to him.

As Mr. Baldwin headed back to his camper, he walked several steps without his cane. Then, he suddenly began hobbling again. He got in the truck, fired up the engine, and then he was gone. Charlie stood there with a look on his face like he was sick.

I walked over to Charlie and asked, "Are you okay?"

Charlie nodded, then ran his hands over his head.

"Your dad sure came and left in a hurry."

"He was too embarrassed to stay."

"Embarrassed?"

Charlie nodded again. "He thought Coach Ryan was dead."

"You mean, he's *not* dead?"

Charlie nodded, breathed in slowly, then exhaled quickly.

I was so relieved, it almost didn't occur to me to ask, "Why did your dad think the coach was dead?"

He shrugged, kicked at some loose sod at his feet, then walked away.

While I stood there watching Charlie disappear into the crowd, I noticed Rocky Whitehead talking to his mom. Mrs. Whitehead looked worried. Rocky was still trying to look tough, but I could tell that something was bothering him, too. When he left his mom's side, I trotted after him.

I called out, "We've sure got a hard game ahead of us."

Rocky paused, as if he was having trouble deciding

whether or not to answer, then he stopped and said, "Yeah. Hard game."

I figured that if I asked Rocky where his dad had been and where he'd gone to now, he probably wouldn't answer. So, I thought I'd try to get him to volunteer the information. I looked down and said, "I sure wish my folks could be here."

Rocky just stood there.

I bit my lower lip and said, "They're in India, you know."

He nodded but didn't say a word.

"You're sure lucky to have both of your parents here cheering you on." I paused a moment, then asked, "Your dad will be back in time for the game, won't he?"

Rocky shrugged, then he said, "See ya, Zeke."

I spoke again before he had a chance to walk away. "Do you think we'll still be in the tournament after the game with the Hurricanes?"

Rocky frowned. "Without Coach Ryan? Or Mr. Crow? Or Ian?" He shook his head. "It'll take a miracle."

Chapter Eleven

The game was starting in twenty minutes, and Dr. Gao hadn't made it back to the fields yet. I was walking behind Mrs. Whitehead and some of the other team moms when I noticed that one of my shoelaces had come undone. As I knelt there to tie it, I heard Rocky Whitehead's mom say, "Ladies, I need to tell you something. As you know, Seth Crow's room was next door to Luke's and mine. Last night, just before we left to go to dinner, we heard voices coming from Seth's room. It sounded like Seth was... *arguing* with Ryan O'Connor." One of the women covered her mouth and made a sound like she was surprised. Mrs. Whitehead then said, "I told the police, so I guess there was nothing else I could have done. It just never occurred to me that Seth Crow would come back and try to–" One of the other moms exhaled, "Shhhh!" I looked up from my still-undone shoelace to see the group of team moms staring down at me. I quickly tied it and joined the other Sundogs.

Mrs. Gao called the Sundogs together and started putting us through our warm-up exercises. Some of my teammates whispered among themselves that they'd rather forfeit to the Miami Hurricanes than play under a woman coach. Pow Wow heard, and his face turned really red. I was going to go over and cheer him up, but before I could take a step, Rocky Whitehead was there beside him whispering in his ear. I figured Rocky was saying something mean to Pow Wow to prove to the other kids that he wasn't soft on the inside like Creamy Puffs cereal.

Enough was enough. Pow Wow was my friend, and I wasn't going to stand by and watch someone mistreat him. I walked over to tell Rocky to leave him alone. When I got there, though, I saw that both Rocky and Pow Wow were smiling. There were times when Uncle Dane made me mad, the way he was always right. Things *weren't* always what they seemed.

Dr. Gao reached us a few minutes later. Everyone asked him about Coach Ryan, Ian Crow and Ian's dad, but all he would tell us was that the coach's condition was unchanged. He said that we should just focus on the game ahead. He was right, I knew, but I couldn't help thinking about what had happened to Coach Ryan. Someone had shot him, and that someone wasn't Mr. Crow. It could have been Mr. Whitehead or Mr. Baldwin who pulled the trigger, but I hadn't been able to find out where either of them had been last night, or this morning. I was so preoccupied that I found myself standing up while all my teammates were down on the ground around me stretching out for the game.

When we huddled up on the sidelines, Dr. Gao told us to get out there and win this one for Coach Ryan. It was bad enough, our going into the game without our coach. Now we wouldn't have our best player, Ian Crow, either. Not only that, but our next-best coach, Mr. Crow, was in jail. All of this when we were facing the Miami Hurricanes – the team that had knocked the Sundogs out of the tournament last year. Even so, Dr. Gao said that we should get out there and give it our best shot. With Charlie Baldwin and me playing forward, we went to work.

For all of the first half and most of the second, things didn't go very well for the Sundogs. Dr. Gao had played soccer when he was younger and he was trying to do his best, but he didn't seem to remember much about the game. With five minutes left in the game, one of the Hurricanes fell and hurt his ankle, so the referee stopped play. The Hurricanes were ahead, 3-1. I'd scored once, but it wasn't enough. Charlie Baldwin had made five attempts on goal, but not a single shot went in. That wasn't like Charlie. He normally would have scored at least once on that many shots. His game was off. I figured it had something to do with what his dad had said to him earlier.

Dr. Gao moved Charlie back to sweeper and had Rocky Whitehead come forward. Play started again. The Hurricanes had possession, but Pow Wow Gao made a bold move and stole the ball. He quickly ran it upfield and passed to Rocky. Fast as lightening, Rocky zigzagged around three of the Hurricanes, but he still didn't have a clear shot.

I faked right, left, then right again, and I was suddenly in the open. I called out, "Switch it!"

Rocky knocked the ball over to me. I took it to the goal. The player guarding me was fast. I was faster. By the time I was within striking distance, there was only one defender left between me and the net. I pulled back the ball with the outside of my right foot. I made it look like I was going to cross it back to Rocky, but I wasn't. The defender fell for it, though, and as soon as he started out across the field, I dribbled as fast as I could toward the goal. I kicked the ball hard. It went past the goalie and slammed into the upper left corner of the net.

I tensed up, waiting for today's ref to call another offside, but there was no whistle. My shot was good. The score was 3-2. Now the Sundogs were only down by one point. There was still a chance for us.

The Hurricanes had the ball, but only for a few seconds. Pow Wow Gao showed his skills again by regaining possession. He rushed the ball back upfield then passed it off to Charlie Baldwin. Charlie just stood there like he didn't know what to do. One of the Hurricanes' midfielders swooped in and stole the ball. I couldn't imagine what Mr. Baldwin could have said to make Charlie act like that.

Rocky Whitehead got in there and, doing some more fancy footwork, took the ball away. After dribbling it up the field once more through a thick patch of Hurricanes, Rocky darted past Charlie then kicked the ball to me. When I turned around, I was facing a wall of Hurricane defense. They were determined not to let me score again. I glanced over to see Pow Wow Gao. He was wide open. I sent the ball flying over the defenders' heads and into the empty space. Pow Wow received it, dribbled twice, then kicked. It went right past the goalie and into the net.

It was 3-3, a tie game.

The parents on the sidelines started chanting, "Sundogs! Sundogs!"

Just then, I glanced over at the players' sidelines and saw something I wouldn't have expected to see. Ian Crow was standing there… in uniform! Dr. Gao spoke to him a moment. I saw Ian nod. Dr. Gao smiled.

Dr. Gao pulled Charlie Baldwin from the game, dropped Rocky back to sweeper again, then pushed Ian onto the field. The last few seconds of the game began to tick away. The Hurricanes took their kick, but Rocky got in there, stole the ball, and brought it back upfield.

I had two defenders on me, but I looked over to see that Ian was wide open. I motioned for Rocky to pass the ball to Ian, but he kicked it to me anyway. I couldn't understand why he'd done that, but there was no time to think. There were only a few seconds left, and I didn't have a shot. There was only one thing I could do. I crossed the ball to Ian. My kick was off, so Ian had to run fast to keep it from going out of bounds. He recovered quickly, drove it up the line, then put it up and scored. The ref blew the long whistle to signal the end of the game.

The Sundogs had won! Normally, the whole team would have crowded around the player scoring the winning goal, especially when that goal had put us into the quarter-finals. That was not the case this morning. Only Dr. Gao, Pow Wow, and I went over to congratulate Ian.

After we stretched and cooled down, Dr. Gao held a short team meeting. He said we'd really shown our stuff by beating the Hurricanes, but I knew that their game had been off. Otherwise, they would have beaten us. Dr. Gao told us that our next game would be at 4:00 that afternoon, against the Cincinnati Sabers. *The Sabers!* Last year, they'd lost the championship to the Sherman Oaks Generals by one goal in overtime. Dr. Gao told us to eat lunch then go back to our rooms to rest up.

Once we broke huddle, everyone started heading for the parking lot. Everyone except Ian Crow, that is. He just walked away alone toward the motel fence. Dr. Gao looked at me, then nodded his head in the direction Ian was heading. I took off after Ian.

Chapter Twelve

No matter how much I tried to get Ian to talk, he just kept walking without saying a word. When we reached the motel fence, he slung his team bag over his neck and started to climb over. I grabbed his shoulder to stop him.

He looked at me. Tears were running down his face. He said, "Let me go, Zeke."

"All right." I took my hand away and stepped back. "Can we talk for a minute first, though?"

"Why? So you can tell me what an awful guy my dad is?" Ian wiped his cheeks on his shirtsleeve. "Well, I've already heard that from the police and everyone else." He turned away.

I bit my lower lip, then said, "You don't think your father shot Coach Ryan, do you?"

He looked back at me and shook his head.

"Well, I don't either."

When I said that, Ian's face brightened.

"I'm going to try to help him. The thing is, I need you to help me first."

Ian looked away again, and he said, "We're just kids, Zeke. You can't help my dad. No one can."

If I told Ian who my uncle really was, who *I* really was, he'd probably have more faith in me. Either that, or he'd think I was pulling another prank. For the time being, it seemed easier to avoid the subject, so I said, "Ian, if there's a chance I could help your dad, don't you think it would be worth trying?"

He looked at me for a moment, then nodded like he wasn't quite convinced.

I smiled and gave him what Uncle Dane liked to call a "you-can-trust-me-so-why-don't-you-just-go-ahead-and-spill-your-guts" look.

It worked. Ian took a deep breath and asked, "How can you help?"

"There are a few things I need to know. Where was your dad last night?"

"In his room."

"All night? Even while we were at dinner?"

Ian nodded.

"How about this morning, when Coach Ryan was shot?"

Ian ran his hands back through his long black hair and said, "He said he'd gotten up early and was just out driving around."

"Did he say why he was in the coach's room in the hospital?"

Ian nodded. "He'd gone there to tell him he was sorry. Dad was afraid Coach Ryan would die before he had a chance to apologize."

"Apologize? For that argument they'd had?"

Ian's mouth hung open. "How'd you know about that?"

"Something I overheard. Do you know what they were arguing about?"

Ian shrugged.

I took a quick breath and said, "Why the disguise?"

Ian cocked his head to the side. "Huh?"

"Why was he dressed up like a surgeon?"

"Oh. He'd tried to get in to the ER see the coach, but they wouldn't let him. He put on scrubs so he could slip past the nurses."

I swallowed hard, then I asked the hardest question. "Why was your dad holding a pillow over Coach Ryan's face?"

Ian looked down, and his hair covered his eyes. "The nurse's finding him there like that was just a misunderstanding."

More than anything, I wanted to know what Ian meant. But I was afraid to say anything for fear that Ian might clam up. So, I did what Uncle Dane told me to do when I wanted someone to talk – I kept my mouth shut.

Ian sniffled and wiped his eyes with the backs of his hands. After waiting a few moments – for me to say something, most likely – he continued, "When Dad walked in, that pillow was on Coach Ryan's face. He was pulling it off when the nurse walked in."

I believed what Ian was telling me. At least, I believed that *he* believed what he was telling me. If what he said was true, then someone else had tried to smother Coach Ryan with that pillow. Most likely, it was the same person who had shot him. The question that remained was: Who?

I bit my lower lip for a moment, then asked, "Do you think you could get me in to see your dad?"

Ian shook his head. "The police called my mom. She'll be here this afternoon. She's taking me back to Dallas. We're leaving right after the four o'clock game."

"If you leave…" I almost said that there would be no way we could win the tournament, but I knew that would only make him feel worse. So, I finished the sentence by saying, "You take it easy."

Ian didn't say a word. He grabbed the framework of the fence and climbed over. I knew better than to leave him alone, so I followed.

Chapter Thirteen

Back in our motel room, Ian didn't say a word. He just sat there on his bed, reading *Ezekial Tobias and the Lost Inca Gold*. That made me uncomfortable. All he'd have to do was look carefully at the picture of the man in sunglasses on the back cover. Then, as Uncle Dane would say, the cat would be out of the bag. My uncle said a lot of things that sounded silly, even if they were true.

An hour later, Mrs. Gao brought us hamburgers and some fries. I thanked her. Ian thanked her. Then she left, and the silence returned.

Some time after that, there was another knock on the door. I opened it. Dr. Gao stood there, pointing at his watch. "The team's meeting downstairs in forty-five minutes. You guys doing okay?"

I nodded.

Ian just sat there on his bed, looking down at his book.

Dr. Gao stuck his head inside the room. "How's it

going, Ian?"

He shrugged.

"I just spoke to your mom. She should be here by halftime."

Ian looked up. "Are we still leaving after the game?"

Dr. Gao nodded. "Sorry, pal. Anything I can do?"

Ian shook his head.

"I'm sorry about the whole situation, Ian. Really, I am."

"My dad didn't shoot Coach Ryan. And he didn't try to suffocate him, either."

When Dr. Gao finally spoke, he said, "I'm sure things will turn out for the best in the end."

Ian looked down at his book, but I had a feeling he wasn't really reading anymore.

"Just get out there this afternoon and give it your best shot, Ian." Before he walked away, Dr. Gao added, "I know your… parents and Coach Ryan would want you to."

As soon as the door shut, Ian pulled his duffel bag out of the closet and began packing.

Chapter Fourteen

The sun was beating down hard. It was hot – African jungle hot – and we were sweating before we'd even begun our warm-ups. Dr. Gao gathered the team together and explained that Coach Ryan's condition hadn't changed. He then said that we should observe a minute of silence for the coach. Afterwards, we Sundogs decided that we would get out there and play our best game ever.

We did.

Dr. Gao tried his best, but he just didn't understand the strategy of soccer. Even so, we played well against the Cincinnati Sabers. Rocky Whitehead kicked in a goal. I netted the ball once as well. In spite of – or maybe because of – his father being in jail, Ian played the best game of his life. He scored twice in the first half. Our defense held the Sabers to zero.

After halftime, just before play began again, I looked over to see Mrs. Jennings, Ian's mom, standing there on the sidelines. Her new husband wasn't with her. Just a few feet away from Mrs. Jennings stood… the man in the black hat, the man who'd been talking to Mr. Crow yesterday afternoon when Coach Ryan got red-carded. I wanted to ask Ian who the man was, but was afraid it would only make him nervous.

During the second half, Ian scored once more. When the referee blew the whistle for the end of the game, the score was 5-0. We had shut out the Cincinnati Sabers. The Dallas Sundogs were advancing to the semi-finals. We would play the Sherman Oaks Generals – last year's champions – at eleven o'clock tomorrow morning.

That was one of those times when I wished my parents could be there to see me. There were a lot of times like that. I missed Mom and Dad. Even though it was a happy moment, I felt sad. The Dallas Sundogs were going up against the Sherman Oaks Generals, and my parents wouldn't be there to see it. Neither would Uncle Dane. Or Ian Crow.

All at once, I felt even sadder. Without Ian Crow, the Sundogs didn't stand a chance.

From the mood of the team in the post-game huddle, everyone else obviously was thinking what I was thinking. Then, while we were stretching out and discussing what we did – right and wrong – in the game, I glanced over to see the mysterious man standing right next to Mrs. Jennings. He'd taken off his black hat and was speaking on his mobile phone. A couple of minutes later, I noticed him talking to Mrs. Jennings. She was shaking her head, like she was answering no.

Just before I turned away, I saw her nod yes.

I wondered if maybe…

After the game, Mrs. Gao called the team and the parents together at the edge of the parking lot. I looked around and noticed Ian Crow talking to his mother over next to her car. I hoped I was right about what I'd seen. During the meeting, we decided to get cleaned up and go to dinner at a Tex-Mex restaurant that Mrs. Gao's cousin had recommended. Since the intensive care waiting room was small, Dr. and Mrs. Gao would go by the hospital to check on Coach Ryan and the O'Connors. Afterwards, they would go to the restaurant and give everyone else a full report. As the team and the parents began to scatter, I looked around and noticed that Mrs. Jennings' car was gone. Neither she nor Ian were anywhere to be seen.

Chapter Fifteen

It was hot, Pow Wow and I had played hard, and we were tired after our game. Even though it was a twenty-minute drive, we decided to ride with his parents from the field to the motel. Mrs. Gao drove fast, as usual. Dr. Gao kept telling her to slow down, but she just patted his hand and told him that she had it under control. At one point, Dr. Gao passed her his keys and told her that *she* ought to be driving the Corvette. I wished he'd give *me* the keys. Mrs. Gao laughed and pitched the keys back into his lap and told him her minivan was faster. Dr. Gao and Pow Wow laughed along with her, and I soon found myself laughing as well. As Mrs. Gao wheeled the minivan into the parking lot, Dr. Gao's mobile phone began to ring. Pow Wow and I got out as he answered. I went up to my room.

Ian Crow was sitting on the corner of his bed, his duffel bag at his feet. His mom stood next to the television.

Mrs. Jennings pulled her long, dark hair back behind her head and said, "Hi, Zeke. How are you?" She sounded nice enough, but I could tell she wasn't very happy.

"Hello, Mrs. Jennings," I replied. "I'm fine. How are you?"

"I've been better." She gave a thin smile. "Good game out there."

I bit my lower lip, then said, "Thanks."

She looked at her son, then put her hands on her hips. "Ian wants to stay and finish the tournament. Mr. Rhea wants him to stay."

I asked, "Who's Mr. Rhea?"

"The man in the black hat standing with me on the sidelines. He's a scout from Everdine."

I'd heard a lot about Everdine. "The prep school out in California?"

Mrs. Jennings nodded. "A lot of their students go to Stanford after graduation. Ian's father convinced Mr. Rhea to come to the tournament so that he could have a look at Ian. Ian's up for a soccer scholarship to Everdine. Mr. Rhea was supposed to return to San Francisco this morning, but his flight was cancelled so he came back to the field to have one more look at Ian. This time, he liked what he saw." She paused and looked over at her son.

My mind shifted into high gear. Ian hadn't scored once during the game with the Buccaneers yesterday afternoon. Coach Ryan took away Ian's last chance to make a shot on goal and gave it to me. My kick was called offside. That shot ended up getting Coach Ryan kicked off the field. The man in the black hat – Mr. Rhea, the Everdine scout – never got a chance to see how good Ian was. No wonder Mr. Crow had been so angry. That must have been what the argument last night in Mr. Crow's room had been about.

Detective García and the police figured Mr. Crow was angry enough to try to kill Coach Ryan for ruining Ian's chance for a scholarship at Everdine. That would explain why Detective García wouldn't take me seriously on the phone.

When Mrs. Jennings spoke again, it half-startled me. "Ian has a good chance of getting that soccer scholarship, but Mr. Rhea wants him to play through the tournament." Mrs. Jennings gave a thin smile and shook her head. "How about you, Zeke?"

I smiled. "I want him to play through the tournament, too."

"Well, then, I guess that makes it unanimous."

Mrs. Jennings had one condition on Ian's continuing in the tournament. That was that he stay with her at her mother's house a few blocks away from the motel. Ian didn't seem very happy about it, but he finally decided that it would be better than going back to Dallas.

Pow Wow Gao saw Ian leaving with his mother and asked if he could move in with me since he was sharing a room with Rocky Whitehead and one of the other players. Ian gave him the key, then he and Mrs. Jennings left. Pow Wow piled his stuff in our room.

We got showered and changed, and I used the blow dryer Ian had left behind to try to flatten my cowlick. It didn't work. We then went down to meet Dr. and Mrs. Gao at the minivan. I looked around for Mr. Whitehead's new white SUV and Mr. Baldwin's camper truck as we walked through the parking lot. Neither was there.

Where were Rocky's and Charlie's dads?

Why did they keep disappearing?

Chapter Sixteen

Dr. and Mrs. Gao walked ahead of us down the long hospital corridor. Pow Wow and I were trying to be quiet, but our tennis shoes squeaked loudly on the polished floor. When we reached the ICU waiting room, we found Mrs. O'Connor sitting there alone, clutching at a handkerchief and dabbing her eyes.

Pow Wow and I glanced at each other. I was afraid something really bad had happened to Coach Ryan. Pow Wow looked as if he thought the same thing.

Mrs. Gao sat down beside Mrs. O'Connor and asked, "What's wrong, dear?"

Tears streaming down her face, Mrs. O'Connor replied, "Nothing!"

"Then why are you crying?"

"I'm just so happy…"

Mrs. Gao sat up straight and put her hand on Mrs. O'Connor's shoulder.

Mrs. O'Connor sniffled, then said, "Ryan woke up! It was only for a minute, but he woke up and saw me and called me 'Mom!'" More tears rolled down her cheeks.

Pow Wow and I looked at each other, smiling. This was the best news possible. For one thing, it meant Coach Ryan was getting better. For another, it meant that he would be able to tell the authorities who shot him.

I knelt beside Mrs. O'Connor and asked, "Have you called the police? They'll want to question—"

"Not now, Zeke!" Mrs. Gao gave me a stern look.

"But—"

"*Not now!*"

I went back over to where Pow Wow was standing. He wouldn't even look at me.

Mrs. Gao patted Mrs. O'Connor on the hand and asked, "Where's your husband?"

"Patrick's in the room with Ryan." Mrs. O'Connor dabbed at her eyes. "The doctor said he only wanted one of us in there with him at a time."

Mr. O'Connor came out to the waiting room. He looked very grim.

Mrs. O'Connor stood so quickly, she almost knocked

Mrs. Gao off of her chair. Mrs. O'Connor hurried to her husband and asked, "What is it? What's wrong?"

He put his arm around her and replied, "Nothing. Nothing at all." He smiled at her, then at the rest of us. "Ryan's going to be just fine. He woke up again. He talked to me! Said he had a headache as big as San Antonio."

Mrs. O'Connor asked, "Can I go in now?"

Mr. O'Connor shook his head. "The doctor said Ryan needs rest. Just those few words tired him out so much he had to go back to sleep."

I stepped forward and asked, "Did he say who shot him?"

The Gaos and the O'Connors stared at me. They had the strangest expressions on their faces. I glanced back at Pow Wow. He was giving me the same look.

Obviously, everyone believed Mr. Crow was guilty. Obviously, none of them had considered the possibility that he might be innocent.

Chapter Seventeen

On the way to the restaurant, I sat alone on the third seat in back of Mrs. Gao's minivan. Nobody said much to me. I guess they figured I was plain *loco*. We passed our motel on the way from the hospital to dinner. The parking lot was empty. That meant everyone was already at the restaurant.

As we continued down the highway, I tried again to figure out who shot Coach Ryan. I couldn't think of any reason that either Mr. Whitehead or Mr. Baldwin would have for trying to kill the coach.

All at once, I had a bad feeling. Whoever shot the coach had tried to suffocate him in the emergency room. Whoever held that pillow over his face was still running around free. Whoever'd done it could come back and try to finish off Coach Ryan.

"Dr. Gao?"

"Yes, Zeke," he answered.

"I think you should call the hospital and have them

put a guard outside Coach Ryan's door."

He and Mrs. Gao exhaled loudly. Dr. Gao turned in the front passenger seat and looked back at me. "Look, Zeke, we've all been through a lot. Seth Crow has been arrested for trying to kill Ryan. No matter how hard it is to believe, the police have their man. Ryan is safe. Could you please just give the tall tales a rest?"

Pow Wow wouldn't even look back at me.

I had to figure it out, and I had to do it fast. Who'd been trying to kill the coach? Mr. Whitehead? Mr. Baldwin?

I'd only seen Rocky Whitehead's dad once since last night. He arrived at the soccer field this morning wearing the clothes he'd had on at dinner. His left hand was now bandaged when it hadn't been last night. Then, as soon as he arrived, he left.

Since the game yesterday afternoon, I'd only seen Mr. Baldwin once, and that was when he thought Coach Ryan was dead. There hadn't been a sign of him since he'd learned that the coach was still alive.

Both men were acting suspicious, but there could have been a million reasons for that. Acting suspicious wasn't a crime, but trying to kill a soccer coach was.

Chapter Eighteen

Hasta la Vista was a brightly painted Tex-Mex restaurant. Its interior walls were covered with colorful striped blankets. Piñatas in the shapes of donkeys and wide-brimmed hats hung from the ceiling. A spicy aroma wafted from the kitchen, and a strolling mariachi band filled the dining room with music.

The team had taken a group of tables on the far side of the restaurant. Even if Pow Wow thought I was crazy, he asked me to sit with him. Rocky Whitehead and Charlie Baldwin were at the next table. Ian Crow was missing, but I figured he was having dinner with his mom at his grandmother's house.

The team parents sat at the big table in the middle of the restaurant. Mrs. Whitehead was there, but her husband wasn't. When the Gaos joined the other parents, Dr. Gao sat and Mrs. Gao clanged a spoon against a glass of ice water. The restaurant grew quiet. She announced, "Sundogs, I have some excellent news. Coach Ryan has woken up!"

Sounds of happiness echoed around the restaurant. Mrs. Gao had to clang on the glass several more times to quiet us down. "He's still very tired, and he can't talk much without wearing himself out, so he can't have any visitors for a while. Even so, it's great news. He's on the road to recovery."

After I'd finished my chicken fajitas, I looked over at the parents' table and noticed that Mrs. Whitehead had left. Where had she gone? I walked over to the table where Rocky and Charlie were sitting.

"Hey, guys."

Rocky didn't look up from the plate of enchiladas he was eating. "Hey, Armstrong."

Charlie Baldwin said, "Hey."

In normal situations, I would never ask rude questions. This was not a normal situation – there was no time to waste. I looked at Charlie and asked, "I haven't seen your dad around lately. Where'd he run off to?"

Charlie shrugged, then he stood and walked away.

"I'll save you the trouble of asking." Rocky dropped his fork in his plate and looked up at me. "My dad's working, and my mom wasn't feeling well, so she went back to the motel." Rocky pushed out a chair with his foot and asked, "Wanna sit?"

I spun the chair around, straddled the seatback, and said, "Thanks."

"Good game today, Armstrong."

"You, too." I paused for a moment, then asked, "Heard much about the Generals?"

He frowned and shook his head. I wondered what he'd do if he knew that *I* was the one who'd left the box of Creamy Puffs cereal in his bag. I knew that my conscience would nag me until I told Rocky I'd been responsible. One of these days, I'd have to apologize. Today wasn't the day, though. I took a deep breath and asked, "So... what *do* you know about the Generals?"

Rocky looked down at the half-eaten taco on his plate, then said, "They have good ball-handling skills, and I hear that they run four miles before every practice. With the hills out there, they're probably the fittest team here."

"They'll be difficult to beat," I agreed.

Rocky nodded, then he grinned. "The thing is, I hear they're not getting much sleep at night."

"How do you know that?"

"I don't think I'm supposed to say anything about this, but…"

Keeping quiet had worked on Ian Crow. I could only hope it did the trick with Rocky Whitehead. I sat there and kept my mouth shut.

"Remember at dinner last night, when my dad got that call and left?"

Of course I remembered. Even so, I didn't want Rocky to know. So I just shrugged and acted like I didn't care.

"Well, his warehouse here in Houston had been burglarized last night. Someone stole a lot of expensive equipment. Millions of dollars worth. My dad was there all night, and he's been there most of today trying to figure out what's missing. He told my mom it has all the markings of an inside job."

I knew what an inside job was, but I didn't want Rocky to know that I knew, so I played dumb. "What's an inside job?"

"Whoever stole all the stuff worked for my dad's company."

My gut was telling me that the burglary was somehow connected to what happened to Coach Ryan. I wanted to know more, but I was afraid of saying the wrong thing. I just sat there, waiting for Rocky to say something else. He didn't. In fact, he started to look uncomfortable, like he was about to stand up and walk away. I gave up the silent act before Rocky started back in with the tough-guy act. "So, what's this got to do with the Sherman Oaks Generals not getting any sleep?"

"You know all the road construction going on around here?"

I nodded.

"My dad's warehouse is next door to the motel where the Generals are staying. The road crews worked straight through the night on the road right in front the motel." Rocky smiled. "They're using jackhammers."

I had a lot of unanswered questions. Had Mr. Whitehead been alone since he left the team dinner last night? Could he have held Coach Ryan hostage and then shot him this morning? If so, why would he do something like that? Because he thought the coach had stolen the equipment from the warehouse? No. It didn't make sense.

There were a lot of things I wanted to know. If I

asked, though, Rocky would probably get suspicious. I could think of only one question that wouldn't sound like I suspected Mr. Whitehead of hurting Coach Ryan. "What happened to your dad's hand?"

Rocky scrunched up his face and cocked his head to one side. "How'd you know about that?"

"This morning, when he came out to the fields, his left hand was all bandaged."

"Oh." He seemed to relax. "He cut it on something in the warehouse. It needed eight stitches. He had to go to the emergency room."

"The one where they took Coach Ryan?"

Rocky nodded. "He was there the whole time, and my mom and I didn't even know." His face scrunched up again, then he said, "You won't tell, will ya Armstrong? My mom told me not to say anything to anyone about any of this. I probably shouldn't have told you."

"I know how to keep a secret, Rocky." And that was the truth. I'd been carrying around a pretty big secret ever since I moved to Dallas.

As I walked away, I was so dazed by what Rocky had told me, I bumped into one of the waitresses. She almost dropped the enormous tray of food she was carrying over her head. I apologized, and she said it was alright. I could hardly believe it. Mr. Whitehead had been in the emergency room – behind those "No Admittance" doors – while Coach Ryan was there. That meant he could have been the one who tried to suffocate the coach with that pillow.

Chapter Nineteen

Dr. Gao's keys jangled in his pocket as we walked through Hasta la Vista's parking lot toward Mrs. Gao's minivan. The green neon lining the edges of the restaurant buzzed in the night. The smell of Mexican food was just as strong as it had been inside. I noticed that Mrs. Gao was carrying a large plastic bag. She said it was dinner for Mr. and Mrs. O'Connor.

We drove past the motel again on our way back to the hospital. The moment we reached the intensive care waiting room, I knew something was wrong. Mr. and Mrs. O'Connor were standing in the corner. She was wringing her hands. He had his arm around her waist, apparently holding her up. They both appeared frantic.

Mrs. Gao handed the bag of food to Pow Wow, then she and Dr. Gao walked over to them. Pow Wow hung back, but I followed. Mrs. O'Connor looked at Mrs. Gao and sobbed, then said, "If anything happens to him, I just don't know what I'll do."

"There, there, Mary." Mr. O'Connor pulled her into a close hug. "He'll be fine. I know he will."

Just then, a doctor walked through the stainless-steel doors and put his hand on Mr. O'Connor's shoulder. "It's a good thing you walked in when you did. Otherwise…"

I stepped up and asked, "What happened?"

Mrs. Gao shot me that disapproving look again, but Dr. Gao nodded and said, "Yes, please, tell us what happened."

The doctor paused, but when the O'Connors nodded at him, he said, "We found Ryan on the floor. He must have tried to get out of bed. When he did, his tubing didn't break free as it should have. I don't understand it. Nothing like that has ever happened here before. It ripped the I.V. right out of his arm."

Mrs. O'Connor gasped.

Dr. Gao asked, "How is he?"

The doctor replied, "Ryan has lost a lot of blood. Such a strange, freakish accident."

I was certain that it wasn't an accident. Someone was trying to kill Coach Ryan. That someone wasn't Ian Crow's father. The question that remained was this: Who? Right now, though, that didn't matter. Coach Ryan needed protection.

I knew the look I'd get from Mrs. Gao, but Coach Ryan's life was worth my getting into trouble. As the doctor turned to walk away, I called out to him. He stopped and turned. I said, "What happened wasn't an accident. Someone's still trying to kill Coach Ryan. You need to put a guard at his door to keep whoever it is from trying again."

Mrs. O'Connor gasped and seemed to go weak in the knees. Mr. O'Connor caught her before she could fall. Dr. and Mrs. Gao looked at me. It felt like their eyes were cutting me in half.

In a controlled tone that sounded much more angry than her angry tone, Mrs. Gao said, "Zeke, you're worrying the O'Connors." She then called past me. "Son?"

Pow Wow replied, "Yes, Mom?"

"Why don't you take Zeke down to the cafeteria for a soda."

Chapter Twenty

My face was so red, it felt like it might catch on fire. We took the elevator downstairs then made our way through a maze of corridors toward the cafeteria. Pow Wow wouldn't talk to me. When I tried to explain, he just shook his head.

There were two elderly women sitting at a table near the windows. Otherwise, the cafeteria dining room was empty. Even after everything he'd eaten at Hasta la Vista, Pow Wow said he was still hungry. It amazed me that such a little guy could eat more than me. When Pow Wow asked me to save him a seat while he went through the buffet line, I knew he was just trying to get rid of me.

I sat at a dark wood table in the far corner of the dining room and thought about everything that had happened since this morning. Someone other than Mr. Crow – someone who smoked cigars – had held Coach Ryan hostage last night. Someone other than Mr. Crow had shot the coach this morning. Someone other than Mr. Crow had tried to suffocate Coach Ryan with a pillow in the emergency room. That someone had just tried again to kill him. Someone besides Mr. Crow had blood on his hands.

No sooner had I thought that, I put my hand in something thick and sticky. Looking down, I noticed that my palm was covered with something red. It wasn't blood. It was ketchup. A large red blob covered the table just in front of where I was sitting. The wood was so dark that I hadn't noticed it.

I tried to get Pow Wow's attention. He was too busy talking to the woman in the serving line to notice. Figuring the restrooms were nearby, I walked out the cafeteria doors.

The restrooms weren't nearby. I went down one hallway, passing a red emergency telephone on the way, then rounded a corner and walked halfway down another corridor. I passed no one. The only sound I heard was that of my tennis shoes squeaking on the tile floor.

I pushed open the door. It looked like the men's room was empty. All of a sudden, I had a funny feeling. The little hairs on my arms stood on end. I remembered what Mrs. Gao had told us: Use the buddy system. I felt very alone.

Come on, Zeke. Don't be such a wimp.

After washing my hands, I looked in the mirror and noticed that my hair was sticking up in back. Like it always did. I wet my hand, then tried to smooth down the cowlick. It didn't work. As I looked at my reflection and told myself that it didn't matter, I heard something that sounded like rustling clothing. It seemed to be coming from inside the men's room.

I left the water running, then got down on my hands and knees and looked underneath the stalls. No feet. Nothing.

After trying one more time to flatten my cowlick, I cut off the water, grabbed a paper towel from the dispenser and dried my hands. As I pulled open the door, I had another one of those strange feelings. The back of my neck tingled. I looked over my shoulder to see a small piece of green operating room clothing hit the ground at the bottom of the nearest stall.

In that split second, I decided to do something I probably wouldn't if I could do it over again. Instead of walking out into the hall, I stayed inside the men's room and let the door shut. I stood there, silent and waiting.

I could hardly believe what I was doing. Even the Ezekial Tobias in the books would have thought twice before doing something that risky. My heart beat fast. I wondered if it could really be the person who had just tried to kill Coach Ryan. I stood there, waiting for whoever it was to step down off the toilet seat so that I could get a look at his shoes. Shoes were good identifiers. Then, I would run back outside and pick up the red emergency phone I'd seen in the hallway and call for help.

I was so busy watching the bottom of the stall, I almost didn't notice the white baseball cap peeking over the top of the stall. I looked up. A pair of eyes peered out at me from underneath the cap's brim. Whoever it was had gotten a good look at me.

What happened next happened fast – so fast, it seemed like a blur. The stall door flew open with a loud bang. The man in the baseball cap dashed out and ran toward me. He was wearing green surgeon's clothing and one of those surgical masks, so I couldn't tell who he was. He was tall, six feet or better. There were red patches on his clothing – Coach Ryan's blood! He lunged at me. I ducked and rolled into his shins – something I'd picked up in Mongolia. The man's feet flew out from underneath him, and when he hit the floor, he hit hard. I caught a whiff of something on his clothing – cigar smoke. He started to get up. I ran out into the hall, dashed around the corner and skidded to a halt at the red emergency phone. When the operator answered, I shouted, "A man attacked me in the men's room! I think it's the same man who tried to kill Ryan O'Connor."

The operator told me to stay where I was, that she would send security. I heard the approach of fast, squeaking footsteps.

Pow Wow ran down the hall toward me. "What happened, Zeke?"

I covered the mouthpiece of the phone and said, "A man just attacked me in the restroom."

He rolled his eyes at me.

"No! Really! I'm telling the–"

A door banged open around the corner. It was so loud, it made Pow Wow jump.

"That's the guy!" I yelled.

All at once, Pow Wow Gao took off in the direction of the restroom.

"Pow Wow! Don't!" I dropped the phone and sprinted after him. Just before he reached the bend in the hallway, I tackled him to the floor.

"Why'd you do that?" he screamed.

"He's already seen me." My breathing was hard. "I didn't want him to see your face, too."

As the sound of the man's footsteps disappeared down the hall one way, the sound of heavy footsteps rushed up behind us. I looked back to see two uniformed hospital security guards charging down the hall.

"He went that way!"

The guards drew their guns, then ran around the corner.

A few minutes later, the guards returned. One of them carried a piece of green cloth.

"That's what he dropped!" I said.

The two officers looked at each other, then one of them held it up and put it on his head. It was a surgical cap. "Son, there are a lot of people in a place like this who have a perfectly good reason for wearing one of these."

"It was a disguise!" I looked at the two guards, then back at Pow Wow. They were all giving me those funny looks. "He was wearing it when he tried to kill Coach Ryan just a few minutes ago."

The guards shook their heads. "We radioed upstairs.

No one is trying to kill Ryan O'Connor. The guy who shot him is in jail. What happened to his I.V. was an accident."

"We heard him getting away!" I looked back at Pow Wow. "Didn't we?"

Pow Wow shrugged and said, "I heard something. A door banging open, I guess."

One of the guards put his hand on Pow Wow's shoulder and asked, "Did you *see* anything?"

Pow Wow looked down and shook his head.

Chapter Twenty-One

No one said a word to me as we rode back up in the elevator. When the guards, Pow Wow and I stepped out into the waiting area, the O'Connors and Dr. and Mrs. Gao appeared very surprised.

Dr. Gao said, "What on Earth…?"

The guards explained the situation, according to the way they saw it, then left.

I thought about trying to tell the Gaos what had really happened downstairs, but I knew they wouldn't believe me. I only had one choice, and that was to tell them all the truth. After that, they'd take me seriously.

"Dr. and Mrs. Gao, Pow Wow…" I bit my bottom lip. "I've got something to tell you."

They stood there, looking as if they expected me to pull another prank.

"You've all met my uncle. The thing is, you don't know who he really is."

Mrs. Gao said, "Your uncle is Dane Armstrong, the author. He writes suspense novels. A lot of people know who he is, Zeke."

"He *does* write suspense novels, but that's not all he does."

The Gaos shot each other curious glances.

"You know the Ezekial Tobias mystery novels?"

They nodded.

"Uncle Dane writes those, too."

Mrs. Gao put her hands on her hips and said, "The Ezekial Tobias novels are written by Abraham Grey."

"That's Uncle Dane's first and middle name."

Dr. Gao raised one eyebrow.

"When Uncle Dane was a boy, they called him 'Ham' – short for Abraham. The other kids started calling him Danish Ham. Then it was shortened to Dane." After pausing a moment, to let what I'd said sink in, I continued, "My full name is Ezekial Tobias Armstrong. *I'm* Ezekial Tobias. Uncle Dane wrote those books about things that happened to me, about crimes that *I* helped to solve! The president of Peru even gave me the medal of honor, just like in *Ezekial Tobias and the Lost Inca Gold*."

There! I smiled and thought, Now they'll take me seriously.

Then I looked at the faces of the Gaos and the O'Connors. They didn't need to say a word. None of them believed anything I'd said.

I was desperate. "Mrs. Gao, you have Uncle Dane's mobile number. Call him."

She shook her head. "Your uncle is in Europe. It's the middle of the night there, Zeke." Mrs. Gao glanced at her watch. "For that matter, it's pretty late here. Could you please just give it a rest?"

By then, I had lost almost all hope of convincing them. I knew it was probably a lost cause, but I added, "Coach Ryan knows who I really am. Next time he wakes up, you can ask him."

The O'Connors gave me blank looks.

I'd lost them. Nothing I said was going to matter, so I figured I might as well go for broke. I looked at the O'Connors one last time and said, "Even if you don't believe me, please have someone stand guard outside Coach Ryan's room. *Please.* His life is still in danger!"

Mrs. Gao started apologizing to the O'Connors for my behavior, but Dr. Gao hustled me out of the waiting room so fast that she and Pow Wow had to run to keep up.

Chapter Twenty-Two

As we pulled out of the hospital parking lot, a big white SUV raced around Mrs. Gao's minivan. I could see something glowing through the dark-tinted side windows as it passed – a cigar? – but I couldn't see who was driving. There was little to tell it apart from all the other big white SUVs on the road, except for one thing: the last three letters on the license plate were "ETA" – my initials. Mr. Whitehead drove a big white SUV with "ETA" on the license plate.

Could Mr. Whitehead have been the man in the restroom who dropped the surgical mask? Was he the one who'd just tried to kill Coach Ryan by ripping out his I.V.? Had he tried to smother the coach this morning? Did he shoot Coach Ryan?

The hospital was ten miles on the other side of the motel from Hasta la Vista. If Mr. Whitehead was, in fact, driving the SUV, what was he doing at the hospital? I thought about mentioning it to the Gaos, but until Mrs. Gao called

Uncle Dane (and I hoped she'd do so first thing in the morning) nobody was going to believe anything I said. Until then, I just hoped that I had stirred things up enough at the hospital so that they would put a guard on Coach Ryan's door in case Mr. Whitehead or whoever it was came back to try to finish the job he'd started.

Of course, if Coach Ryan lived through the night, my problems were just beginning. In the morning, the Sundogs would have to face the Sherman Oaks Generals with Dr. Gao as our coach. At the same time, *I* would have to face my teammates' taunts and teasing. I imagined that they'd call me Sherlock and pounce on me every time I didn't figure something out. They'd probably be harder on me than they were on Rocky. After all, he never told them he'd been the kid in the Creamy Puffs commercial. Me, I blabbed my secret, like I was bragging about it. I deserved all the ribbing I got. No matter how much I tried to look on the bright side, I just couldn't find one.

Chapter Twenty-Three

When we got back to the motel, Mr. Whitehead's white Expedition was already there, backed into a space in the lot. Mrs. Gao parked next to it. I climbed out of the back door of the minivan and touched the SUV's hood. It was hot to the touch.

The Gaos were busy moving things around in the back of their minivan. I moved around to the driver's side of the Expedition. The window was partially open. I put my nose up next to the crack and took a deep whiff. Cigar smoke! I thought about saying something about it to the Gaos, but decided against it. I was in enough trouble as it was.

As we walked through the parking lot toward the motel, the keys in Dr. Gao's pocket rattled. I looked at the row of windows on the bottom floor. The lights in Mr. and Mrs. Whitehead's room were off. Either no one was there, or the Whiteheads were already asleep. I checked my watch. 8:15 p.m. It seemed awfully early for bedtime. I decided to place an "accidental" wrong-number call to the Whiteheads as soon as I got back upstairs.

Glancing up at my room, I noticed something strange. The curtains parted for a moment, then slowly closed. There shouldn't have been anyone in there. I looked over my shoulder to see Pow Wow dragging behind his parents. Thinking what I saw might have been my imagination, I looked back up at the room and saw the curtains part slightly again.

Someone was in our room. Ian had given Pow Wow his key. Pow Wow was with me. It was much too late for the maid service. My hunch was the person in Pow Wow's and my room was the person who'd been hiding out in the restroom in the hospital, the person who'd been trying to kill Coach Ryan.

Keeping my eyes on my windows, I stopped and waited for Dr. Gao to catch up. I then fell in step with him. Trying my best to keep my voice calm, I whispered, "Dr. Gao, whatever you do, please don't stop walking and don't look up. There's someone in my room."

Keeping his head level, I saw him lift his eyes to room number 211. He seemed to tense as he stared up at the windows for several steps, then breathed a deep sigh and looked over at me. "Zeke, I think we've all had just about enough of this."

"Please, Dr. Gao. I'm serious."

He inhaled slowly, then exhaled quickly. "Zeke…"

I looked up at him and gave him a pleading look.

Dr. Gao shook his head, then finally said, "All right. I'll go up and check it out."

In one of the spaces nearest the motel, I noticed Mr. Baldwin's camper truck. Its hood was partially ajar. There was no one in the vehicle.

Chapter Twenty-Four

Mrs. Gao said she was going to the motel office to check on tomorrow morning's wake-up calls. As Dr. Gao climbed the steps to the second floor, the keys jangled in his pocket. Pow Wow and I followed behind. Pow Wow didn't seem quite sure if he should be afraid, or just annoyed with me. When we reached the top of the stairs and started down the exterior walkway to our room, I got goose bumps.

Stopping outside our door, I handed my room key to Dr. Gao and whispered, "Be careful."

He just smiled back at me. "Zeke, you worry *way* too much for a guy your age."

Dr. Gao unlocked the door and pushed it open. He flipped the light switch. The room stayed dark. "That's funny…" he muttered, "Bulb must have burned out."

He entered the room. As I followed, I noticed a shadow in the corner. It started moving. It was heading for Dr. Gao.

"Watch out!" I screamed.

It was too late. The next thing I knew, Dr. Gao had been shoved back into me. We fell through the door and hit the walkway floor. I was pinned beneath Dr. Gao.

I heard the sounds of a scuffle, then fast, heavy footsteps racing away toward the stairs. By the time I managed to work my head out from underneath Dr. Gao, I caught only a glimpse of the white baseball cap on the head of someone running down the stairs.

When I shook Dr. Gao, he didn't budge. I figured he must have hit his head on the floor and been knocked unconscious. I called out, "Pow Wow! Help!"

He didn't answer.

I looked around. I didn't see him anywhere.

"Pow Wow?" I called out.

All I heard was a muffled scream coming from the bottom of the stairs.

Pow Wow!

I looked down to see a man in a baseball cap running across the parking lot… dragging Pow Wow along behind him.

Chapter Twenty-Five

I worked my way out from under Dr. Gao, then checked to make sure he was still breathing. He was. I noticed a set of keys lying there beside him. *His car keys!* They must have fallen out of his pocket. I grabbed them and raced down the stairs.

As I ran, I called out for Mrs. Gao.

She didn't answer.

Mr. Whitehead's white Expedition started up and the headlights came on.

I yelled, "Help!"

There was no reply.

I dashed out across the lot, toward Dr. Gao's tarp-covered Corvette convertible. The Expedition squealed out of its parking space.

I yanked at the canvas covering the car. The top and the windows were down. I leapt over the door and into the driver's seat.

As the big white SUV sped away toward the parking lot entrance, a blue car pulled in. The Expedition swerved, but it hit the car's front fender. The car went crashing into one of the other parked cars. The SUV paused for a moment, then roared out onto the road.

I fastened my seatbelt, started the car and put it in Drive. As I raced toward the road, I saw Ian Crow and his mother stepping out of the blue car. I slowed down to ask Mrs. Jennings if she was okay.

Her eyes grew wide. "Zeke? What on Earth are you–"

"Dr. Gao's outside my room. He needs help." I pointed at the white Expedition speeding away. "He's got Pow Wow! Call 9-1-1!"

As I hit the gas, Ian jumped over the Corvette convertible's door and into the car with me.

I looked at him and said, "Get out!"

Ian buckled his seat belt.

There was no time to argue. I hit the gas.

Mrs. Jennings ran after us, yelling, "Stop!"

Chapter Twenty-Six

Tires squealed as the convertible fish-tailed out of the parking lot. I eased up on the accelerator and pointed the nose of the car toward the Expedition speeding away into the night. It was very hard to see the road ahead.

Ian called out, "Lights!"

I searched for the switch. When I finally found it, the headlights popped up and I could see again.

Up ahead, the big white SUV turned to the right. Careful to keep my distance, I took the same turn and found myself on the interstate highway access road. The Expedition merged onto the interstate. I did the same.

It had been a year since I'd driven – Uncle Dane didn't think it was a good idea for me to do so in the States – but I remembered what to do. Keeping the car between the lines marked on the road wasn't easy, but pavement was a lot smoother than the dirt roads in the jungle and on the plains.

Over the wind noise, Ian called out, "Who are we chasing?"

"The man who shot Coach Ryan."

"Isn't that…"

"Mr. Whitehead's Expedition." I glanced at Ian, and saw the same look of disbelief that I knew had to be on my face. "I can't believe it either."

"Do you think he…"

I shook my head. "I don't know for sure if it *is* Rocky's dad. I never got a good look at him. It might be Mr. Whitehead. Then again, it might be… someone else."

One thing I *did* know was that we needed to call the police. In fact, that had been my plan – to stay with the Expedition until the police could take over. I reached for my mobile phone, but it wasn't on my waistband. Even the clip was gone. I figured it had gotten knocked off when Dr. Gao fell on top of me.

"Ian, do you have a cell phone?"

He looked at me like I'd asked him if he could fly.

"Maybe Dr. Gao keeps one in his car."

Ian searched every compartment. He found nothing.

"I just hope someone at the motel has Mr.

Whitehead's license number. Otherwise, it's going to be up to us to save Pow Wow."

"Pow Wow?! Where's Pow Wow?"

I pointed at the red taillights piercing the night ahead. "Mr. Whitehead – or whoever that is up there – he's got him. I thought you knew."

Ian shook his head.

"Then why did you jump in the car with me?"

"Are you kidding? I've always wanted to ride in a Corvette." He then cast me a curious look. "Hey, since when do you know how to drive?"

"I learned when I was seven years old. We were living in Tanzania then."

"Tanzania?"

"Yeah. It's in Africa."

"I know where it is. I just didn't realize you'd lived there."

"I've lived lots of places." I named off the seven countries my parents and I had called home.

Ian whistled.

I said, "Look, Ian, this could get dangerous, but there's no time to stop and let you out. We have to stay with them." I paused a moment, then asked, "Why were you and your mom coming back to the motel?"

Ian pulled on his hair, which I now noticed was still wet. "I forgot my blow dryer. Now, you want to fill me in on what's going on?"

As we followed the big white SUV, I told Ian about what had happened at the hospital and then back at the motel.

Chapter Twenty-Seven

As we drove toward the outskirts of the city, humid night air blasted us. Ian's hair dried quickly, and it flew around hitting him in the face until he found a rubber band and pulled it back. I kept hoping we'd see a police car, but we never passed one. I didn't know how long we were going to have to follow the Expedition, so I checked the gas gauge on Dr. Gao's Corvette. The tank was full, and so was the moon overhead.

Soon, we were out in the country. The little traffic that had been on the highway soon dwindled to practically none. I exited onto the access road, followed it for a while, then took the entrance ramp.

Ian called out, "Why'd you do that?"

I pointed at the red taillights ahead. "I don't want whoever that is figuring out that we're following them. Something I picked up in Jakarta."

Ian nodded. "You're a regular Ezekial Tobias." He

smiled. "Ever solve any crimes?"

"Well…" My voice trailed off. I wasn't going to tell Ian, but I figured it was only a matter of time before he found out anyway. "I did help track down some stolen gold in Peru a couple of years ago. The thieves chased me down the side of a mountain in the Andes. The old bus I was driving almost went over a cliff."

Even in the moonlight, I could see the look of realization wash over Ian's face. "Your Uncle Dane is… Abraham Grey."

I nodded.

"You're… the *real* Ezekial Tobias."

I nodded again.

"Why didn't you tell us?"

"After the way you clowns harassed Rocky Whitehead for being in that Creamy Puffs commercial? You've got to be kidding."

Ian shrugged. "Being Ezekial Tobias is cool. We wouldn't razz you about that."

I cast him a sideways glance.

"Well, *I* wouldn't. Anyway, if you're this ace crime-solver, tell me this. If Mr. Whitehead's not driving that big white SUV up there, who is?"

I bit my lower lip, then said, "Well, I know it isn't your father."

Ian laughed out loud and said, "Well, duh, Sherlock!"

I shook my head. "That's exactly why I didn't tell anybody about the Ezekial Tobias books."

"All right, all right. You made your point." Ian looked at me. His face was serious again. "Who do you think that is up there?"

"As best I can figure, if it's not Mr. Whitehead, it's Mr. Baldwin."

"Mr. Baldwin? He can barely walk. How could he have carried off Pow Wow like that?"

"I don't know, Ian. There's just something that's not right here. It's like Uncle Dane says: sometimes things just aren't what they seem."

Chapter Twenty-Eight

I drove a long way, for what seemed like hours. We never passed a police car, and we couldn't risk stopping even long enough to use a pay phone to call the police. The land was flat and, from the lack of lights, it seemed that very few people lived around there. We exited the interstate and then pulled back on a few more times so that whoever it was in the big white SUV wouldn't think we were following them. Once, while there were no other cars on the road, I switched off the headlights and drove by the light of the moon. It wasn't a very safe thing to do, but Pow Wow's life was in danger. I couldn't risk the SUV's driver figuring out we were following him.

Finally, we reached another city. It was hard to tell from the road signs, and we couldn't find a map in the car, but Ian figured it must be Corpus Christi. He remembered Mr. Whitehead mentioning that he'd grown up there. A moment later, Ian told me that Charlie Baldwin had been born in

Corpus Christi.

Instead of going through downtown, we followed the highway around the outskirts of the city. As the lights began to fade away in the distance, the traffic remained thin. I followed the SUV from a distance for several minutes before I noticed it climbing a steep incline.

I nudged Ian and asked, "There aren't any big hills down here, are there?"

He shook his head.

"Then what's that?"

When I looked ahead again, I noticed the lacey metal span with blinking red lights on top.

In a serious tone, Ian said, "That's what we call a bridge, Sherlock."

"Those stupid books!" I shook my head. "I knew it'd be a bad idea for me to tell anyone."

We started up over the bridge. The water below was oily black in the moonlight, and it smelled of salt. We'd reached the Gulf of Mexico. I'd seen all the oceans and a lot of seas, but I'd never been to the Gulf. This wasn't the way I imagined seeing it for the first time.

Soon, we were over the bridge and on an island – a

long, flat, narrow island. After we'd passed dozens of expensive-looking homes lining the beach to the left, the roadside became deserted. The moon was directly overhead, its light very bright. I pulled off on a side road, switched off the headlights, then pulled back onto the highway. The Expedition's taillights still glowed like two red dots ahead of us. I dropped back so that the driver wouldn't see the moonlight shining off of the Corvette's hood.

Sand dunes rose up on the left side of the road. Between the dunes, Ian and I caught glimpses of waves crashing into the beach on the other side. Salty, sandy wind blew in off the Gulf.

The big white SUV's taillights glared bright red, and the vehicle suddenly turned off to the left. I took my foot off of the gas pedal. An engine revved in the distance. A moment later, there was a sound of crashing metal.

Ian and I looked at each other.

I geared down the transmission then used the emergency brake to bring the Corvette to halt without stepping on the brake pedal. I didn't want whoever it was that had Pow Wow to see the brake lights.

I pulled over next to a sand dune, got out of the car

and said, "This could be dangerous. Stay here."

"Yeah, right." Ian jumped out of the car and ran alongside me.

We followed the path the SUV had taken. There was a crumpled gate that had once stood guard over the beach entrance. In the moonlight, we could see that the sign read "Private Property – No Access".

Chapter Twenty-Nine

Large, white-capped waves crashed into the beach. There on the sand near the water's edge stood the white Expedition. Its taillights were glowing red, and the driver's door stood open. Off in the distance, a tall man in a baseball cap was dragging a smaller person down the beach. Over the roar of the waves, I could hear screams. It was Pow Wow. The man was smoking a cigar. I still couldn't tell if it was Mr. Whitehead or Mr. Baldwin. Whoever it was wasn't limping, but I remembered the Gaos saying that Mr. Baldwin might have been faking his injuries.

"There!" I pointed out the figures on the beach.

Ian nodded in reply.

"Pow Wow's alive, but we don't have much time." I looked around for some way of sneaking up on them. The beach was too open. I looked back and said, "The sand dunes!"

Ian and I scrambled over the dunes and moved down

the beach until we were just inland from a long concrete pier that jutted out into the Gulf of Mexico. A large truck had been backed out to the end of the pier. It was hard to see in the night, but I could make out the forms of two or three men in dark clothing milling around the truck. A large boat was moored to the end of the pier.

I looked down as the baseball-capped man and Pow Wow reached the ladder that led up to the top of the pier. The man was pointing something at Pow Wow. He moved it slightly. It glinted in the moonlight. It looked like… a gun!

The baseball-capped man waved the gun toward the ladder. Pow Wow stood his ground there on the beach. The man pointed the gun at the sky and fired a single shot. The loud bang it made could be heard over the roar of the waves. It was the sound I'd heard early that morning as I laced up my shoes on the motel steps. Pow Wow approached the ladder.

I nudged Ian. "The guy in the baseball hat's going to put Pow Wow on that boat." I pointed at the end of the pier. "If Pow Wow gets on that boat, he's as good as dead."

Ian looked at me. He'd lost his rubber band. His long black hair rustled in the salty breeze. "What are we going to do?"

"Stop him."

As I rose to my feet, I heard a loud rumbling sound, one that drowned out the roar of the waves. Pow Wow paused at the bottom of the ladder and looked up. The baseball-capped man looked up, too.

So did I.

A massive, dark, droning thing passed overhead, then hovered above the old concrete pier. All at once, a bright light beamed down from the object. The face of the baseball-capped man was suddenly illuminated. Then I realized how the burglary at Mr. Whitehead's warehouse was connected to the attempts on Coach Ryan's life.

Chapter Thirty

Pow Wow covered his eyes, but Charlie Baldwin's dad just stood there. The wind blew the baseball cap right off of his shaved head. It seemed that he'd been frozen by the light and the noise coming from the helicopter that hovered overhead. After a few moments, he, too, raised his hands and shielded his face. The darkly clad figures at the end of the pier jumped into the large boat, then it began to speed away.

It all made sense. Mr. Baldwin was going to lose his lawsuit against the other driver. He wasn't working. He was out of money. Rocky had said that the burglary of his father's warehouse was an inside job. Mr. Baldwin and the men in dark clothes had broken into the warehouse to find Coach Ryan there, thinking about what he'd done to get red-carded. The expensive equipment that Mr. Baldwin and the darkly clad men had stolen was probably on the boat that was speeding away.

I knew that Pow Wow probably wouldn't be able to

see for a while, after looking into the helicopter's bright light. The good news was, Mr. Baldwin wouldn't be able to see, either. Now was Pow Wow's chance. I tore down the dune yelling, "Run, Pow Wow! Run!"

Ian followed, calling out, "Run!"

Looking over my shoulder, I yelled, "Stay back, Ian!"

I sprinted across the beach, my tennis shoes slipping in the sand, calling out, "Pow Wow, it's Zeke! Run toward my voice!"

Pow Wow dashed out of the pool of light and hurried toward me. From the helicopter droning overhead, a voice blared over the loudspeaker, "This is the police. Drop your weapon and put your hands on your head."

Mr. Baldwin didn't drop the gun. Instead, he pointed it overhead and fired at the helicopter. The bright light suddenly went out.

Then, I was at Pow Wow's side. Even in the wind, I could smell the cigar smoke on him. Taking Pow Wow by the arm, I dashed across the sand toward the dunes. I looked back to see Mr. Baldwin fire overhead again. The helicopter suddenly tilted and raced out across the water in the direction the boat was taking.

Ian was waiting. Together, he and I pulled Pow Wow over the dunes and down to the road. I glanced back. There was no sign of Mr. Baldwin. Over the crash of the waves and the roar of the helicopter, I heard police sirens. They were coming our way, coming to help us. I hoped they would make it in time.

Chapter Thirty-One

I jumped behind the wheel. There was no back seat in the Corvette, so Ian and Pow Wow crammed themselves into the passenger seat. I started the engine and turned on the headlights.

Pow Wow was hysterical. "He was going to kill me! He was going to take me out into the middle of the Gulf and throw me overboard."

I put the car in drive and hit the gas. Tires squealing, I did a U-turn.

Ian called out, "Why are we going back this way?"

"Help." I pointed at the flashing lights of the police cars that appeared in the distance. "Keep your heads down."

The car picked up speed rapidly. For a moment, I thought we were going to be safe. Then, I noticed a ghostly form rising over the top of one of the sand dunes ahead. I hit the brakes as the white Expedition plowed down the side of the dune and skidded to a stop across the road in front of us. As I brought the Corvette to a halt, the SUV's dark glass driver's window glided down. Mr. Baldwin smiled his smile that wasn't a smile at all and pointed the gun at us.

"Hold on, guys!" I put the car in reverse and punched the accelerator. When the car was going fast enough, I cut the wheel to the left and hit the emergency brake. The Corvette's sleek nose traded places with the bumper, and in an instant we were pointing the other direction. I straightened the wheel, released the brake, dropped the transmission back into drive and hit the gas.

As we accelerated away, I could feel Pow Wow's stare.

"Bootlegger turn. Something I picked up in La Paz."

"But…" The frantic expression on Pow Wow's face was suddenly replaced by a look of shock. "You know how to drive?"

Ian pointed at me and said, "He's Ezekial Tobias."

I glanced back. Mr. Baldwin was following us. Moments later, the Expedition's headlights glared in the rearview mirror. Ian and Pow Wow looked back over the top of their seat.

"Get down, guys!" I yelled. "He's got a gun."

Bullets whizzed past us. I pushed the accelerator to the floor. The car took off like it'd been launched from a catapult.

Chapter Thirty-Two

We sped down the flat island road, putting more and more distance between us and the big white SUV. I glanced back to see police cars in the distance. I could only hope they were fast enough to help us.

We turned another curve. I saw flashing red lights ahead and raced toward them. By the time I realized that the lights weren't coming from police cruisers, it was too late to take another road. We were heading for a drawbridge. The crossing gate had already been lowered. It was blocking our path. The bridge was being raised. Off to the right, in the shipping channel, I saw the hulking outline of an enormous oceangoing vessel. It was moving toward the bridge.

The lights of the Expedition grew brighter in the rearview mirror. There was nowhere else to go, nothing I could think of to do. I looked at Pow Wow and asked, "How much does your dad love this car?"

"A lot." His eyes grew wide. "He loves me more."

"Hold on, guys!"

I hit the gas. The car crashed through the gate, then started up the section of iron-grated roadway that was tilting up away from the water. We were driving up a hill that kept getting steeper. I thought surely the operator would see us and stop raising the drawbridge. Still, it kept rising.

Near the end of the section of bridge, I stopped the car. The incline had grown so steep, I didn't know how much longer it would be before the Corvette's tires began to slip on the iron-grate surface. As I switched off the engine and the lights, I looked back to see the big white SUV racing toward the base of the bridge. I yelled at Ian and Pow Wow, "This is where we get out!"

We couldn't open the Corvette's doors at such a steep angle, so we hopped over them. Ian, Pow Wow, and I crab-walked up the steep grade toward the top. Suddenly, we were again awash in light. I looked back to see the Expedition driving up the ramp.

"Faster, guys!"

Chapter Thirty-Three

The white Expedition crashed into the back of the Corvette then came to a halt. Still, the bridge kept rising. Why didn't the operator see what was happening? Why didn't he stop the bridge?

Mr. Baldwin got out of Mr. Whitehead's SUV. He stuck his gun in the waistband of his shorts then started climbing toward us. I heard the sound of skidding rubber. The sleek black Corvette and the big white SUV had begun to slide backwards. Moments later, both vehicles tumbled down the incline and crashed into the ground below. There was an explosion, then both vehicles were on fire.

I glanced to the side and saw that the big container ship was still heading toward us. All at once, I realized why the operator hadn't stopped the bridge. Such an enormous ship couldn't stop very quickly. If the operator stopped the bridge, the ship would hit. Pow Wow, Ian, and I would be goners.

Mr. Baldwin looked up at us and smiled. He got a toe-hold then pulled the gun from beneath his belt and fired.

Another shot whizzed past us.

I shouted, "Take cover!"

The problem was, there was nowhere to hide. Unless…

I climbed over the edge of the rising section of the bridge, grabbed the rib of the metal beam, and dropped. Ian and Pow Wow looked over the top to see that I hadn't fallen off into the water.

"Come on, guys. Hang off!"

They scurried over the top, grabbed hold of the edge of the beam then let their legs dangle above the black water far below.

The bridge kept rising as Ian, Pow Wow, and I held on tight. My fingers burned, and my arms ached. If we fell from that height, I didn't know if we would survive. I looked at Pow Wow to my left and Ian to my right. "You guys okay?"

They nodded, but I could tell they were scared.

I looked past Pow Wow to see that the enormous ship was still heading toward us. If Mr. Baldwin didn't shoot us first, I was afraid that the ship would scrape us off the bridge. I held on, speaking through gritted teeth. "Hold on, guys. Hold on!"

Chapter Thirty-Four

After a few moments that felt like hours, the drawbridge was fully open. Just as the enormous cargo ship reached us, Ian, Pow Wow, and I hoisted our legs up and stood on the beam, which was now horizontal. The big container ship, with the name "Santa Lucia" painted along the bow, began to pass us by. It was enormous, like a skyscraper turned on its side. I noticed the sounds of the sirens, and looked down to see the police had finally arrived.

Were they too late?

I peeked over the edge. Mr. Baldwin was still climbing. He needed both hands to hold on to the bridge, so he'd tucked the gun back into his belt. That would change when he reached the top. If the police couldn't stop him, he'd reach us soon. Enormous, dark, and silent, the container ship passed behind us.

Below, a policeman with a bullhorn shouted, "Bud Baldwin! Stop! This is the police! Drop your weapon and stay where you are!"

Mr. Baldwin reached into his belt and shot at them once. The police didn't return the fire. I wondered why. Then I realized that they couldn't shoot at Mr. Baldwin without risking hitting Pow Wow, Ian, or me. Mr. Baldwin obviously realized this as well, because he tucked the gun back into his waistband and began to climb again.

I looked around. The enormous ship cruised through the passage. It was so quiet. I couldn't believe something that huge could be that quiet. The water churned black far below. Even if we did survive the fall, I figured we'd get sucked into the ship's huge propellers. If we tried to climb down, Mr. Baldwin would shoot at us.

There was nowhere to run, nowhere for us to hide. We had no way to protect ourselves. Once Mr. Baldwin reached the top of the ramp, he would probably shoot us or knock us off into the water. Either way, we'd probably die. There seemed to be nothing we could do.

The police below shouted again, "Bud Baldwin! Stop and think about what you're doing. If you turn yourself in right now, you'll be charged with attempted murder. That's a lot better than murder one! Think about it."

Mr. Baldwin obviously didn't think about it very much. He reached up and grabbed the top of the ramp with one hand. I thought about going over and stomping on it, but a moment later, the other hand was there, holding the gun. Then, we saw the top of his shaved head.

At that moment, I glanced back at the ship. A large expanse of netting hung off the side. It was just a few feet away. I looked at Pow Wow and Ian, and they seemed to understand. We all turned and faced the ship. As Mr. Baldwin hoisted one leg up on the top of the ramp, I cried out, "Jump!"

Chapter Thirty-Five

It was another muggy morning in Houston. The air smelled like freshly mowed grass, and the sidelines were newly chalked. Less than a minute into our game with the Sherman Oaks Generals, Ian Crow scored. Two minutes later, he scored again. A minute after that, I kicked one in. The score was 3-0.

We Sundogs started getting confident, thinking we had this one in the bag.

That's when the Generals came back and blasted four past our goalie.

At halftime, the score was 4-3, Generals. Ian Crow, Pow Wow Gao, and I were really tired after everything that had happened the night before, but we didn't want to miss this game. Neither did Ian Crow's dad. For the first time I could remember, Mr. Crow didn't have a cigarette in his hand. He told us we needed to pick up the intensity if we were going to win this game. We all agreed to give 110% –

even if we knew it was impossible to give more than 100% – in the second half.

On our kick-off, Ian knocked it back to Pow Wow, who put it out wide to Rocky Whitehead. Rocky took it up the line with amazing speed. Ian and I made our runs, and Rocky crossed it in the air to me. I jumped up and headed it towards the goal. It looked like it was going in, but at the last second, the Generals' goalie dove and caught it.

Mr. Crow shouted for us to turn it up another notch. Pow Wow Gao quickly regained control of the ball and passed it to Charlie. He dribbled past three defenders, but he had a bad angle. Charlie hooked his foot around and shot the ball. It bounced off a defender, hit the side post, and went out of bounds. Pow Wow went to take the corner kick. At the last moment, I charged forward, and Pow Wow passed the ball to me. I then crossed it to Ian. He settled the ball and shot. It went right into the goal.

We had a lot of scoring opportunities after that, but we couldn't seem to finish the ball. Fortunately, the Generals weren't able to score either. Late in the second half it was still tied 4-4. The ball went out of bounds off one of the Generals' kicks, so the Sundogs had a throw-in. I took it. Mr. Crow yelled, "Give us a good throw, Zeke!" I was on the parents' sidelines. I should have had my mind on the game, but I couldn't help noticing the man in the black hat – Mr. Rhea, the Everdine scout – standing there with Mrs. Jennings.

The game was at stake, but so was Ian's scholarship. I picked up the ball and motioned for Ian to make a run. He sprinted down the sideline and into the clear. I threw the ball with all my might. It went over the head of the defenders and into empty space. Ian took the ball toward the goal. It was a one-on-one with the goalie. The goalie shifted left. Without hesitation, Ian shot toward the right corner. It went in. The whistle blew.

The Sundogs had won.

We were going to the finals.

Even so, Ian, Pow Wow, Rocky, and the rest of the team walked off the field as if we'd just been shut out by the Generals.

Chapter Thirty-Six

Advancing to the finals was more than the Sundogs could have hoped for, especially after everything that had happened. Even so, we all dragged our feet as we headed off the field. There was too much bad mixed in with the good for us to celebrate.

Coach Ryan was still in intensive care, and, as Dr. Gao had explained before our game with the Generals began, he wasn't out of the woods yet. Mr. Baldwin was in jail for trying to kill Coach Ryan, Pow Wow, Ian, and me, not to mention the theft of millions of dollars worth of medical equipment. The worst part of Mr. Baldwin's arrest was that Charlie Baldwin was now gone. As soon as his grandmother – his mother's mother – heard the news, she drove up to Houston from Corpus Christi and took Charlie home with her. I knew I'd probably never see Charlie again, and I was sad about that. He was a nice guy and a good soccer player.

When Coach Crow finished going over what we'd

done right and wrong in our game with the Sherman Oaks Generals, I looked around for Mr. Rhea, the Everdine scout. I didn't see him anywhere, but I did notice Pow Wow's dad walking toward us.

Dr. Gao walked into the middle of our huddle and said, "Sundogs, when we're done here, we're all going to caravan over to the hospital." His expression was very grim.

Mobile phone clipped to my waistband, I rode to the hospital with the Gaos. Dr. Gao sat there in the front passenger seat of the minivan without saying a word. I'd apologized more than once about wrecking his beautiful car, but he just kept thanking me for saving his son's life and apologizing for not believing me sooner.

On the way to the hospital, I asked Dr. Gao about Coach Ryan, but he wouldn't answer. Then I asked him about Mr. Rhea, the Everdine scout, and whether or not Ian had gotten the scholarship. He still wouldn't answer. I finally gave up on asking questions. I had a feeling this story might not have as happy an ending as *Ezekial Tobias and the Lost Inca Gold*, in spite of all the good that had happened.

Pow Wow, Ian, and I were lucky. Moments after we'd jumped onto the netting, the *Santa Lucia* carried us away from the line of gunfire. The police fired at Mr. Baldwin once, then he surrendered and climbed down. He confessed to everything.

When Mr. Baldwin and his henchmen had broken into the Whitehead Medical Supply warehouse, they found Coach Ryan sitting on a forklift. Mr. Baldwin tied up the coach and left him in the cab of his camper as he and his men filled their truck – the truck I'd seen parked at the end of the pier – with expensive equipment. Then, Mr. Baldwin and his men hid the truck and the camper, along with Coach Ryan, in a self-storage garage a few blocks from the soccer fields.

Mr. Baldwin had sat there smoking cigars all through the night while he waited for morning so that the truck would be less conspicuous. At dawn, Mr. Baldwin dozed off and Coach Ryan managed to loosen the ropes binding his hands. He escaped from the garage and had made it all the way across the soccer fields before Mr. Baldwin caught up with him. Coach Ryan was trying to climb over the motel fence when Mr. Baldwin shot him.

Had the coach not survived the shooting, Mr. Baldwin and his henchmen would have left Houston immediately. As it was, though, Mr. Baldwin decided to stay in town to try to finish off the coach. It was he who had tried to suffocate Coach Ryan with the pillow in the emergency room, and it was also he who had ripped the I.V. out of the coach's arm. Mr. Baldwin was the man in the white baseball cap who'd attacked me in the men's room in the hospital.

While a small Coast Guard boat went out to the *Santa Lucia* to fetch Pow Wow, Ian, and me, one of their big armed cutters headed off the ship that Mr. Baldwin's henchmen had used to transport Mr. Whitehead's medical equipment and forced it back to shore. The one thing I couldn't figure out was how the helicopter had found us. But, as the sheriff who'd driven Pow Wow, Ian, and me back to Houston explained, that was thanks to Mr. Whitehead.

Mr. Baldwin's battery had gone dead, so he abducted Mr. and Mrs. Whitehead and left them bound and gagged in the back of the camper while he stole their Expedition. It was hours before the police found the Whiteheads. When they did, though, Mr. Whitehead had them activate the anti-theft tracking device. He'd had it installed on his vehicle because his last SUV had been stolen. The signal led them straight to that deserted pier near Corpus Christi – just in the nick of time.

Pow Wow and I followed the Gaos to a part of the hospital I didn't recognize. When we reached the end of the corridor, we found some of our teammates and their parents standing there. Some of us boys started talking, but Dr. Gao told us to be quiet. His expression was very serious. A few minutes later, Rocky Whitehead and his parents arrived. You could still see the red marks around Mr. Whitehead's wrists, where Mr. Baldwin had tied him up. Rocky didn't seem to be acting so tough anymore.

I pulled Rocky aside and said, "I put the Creamy Puffs in your team bag."

"I knew you'd done it." Rocky smiled and added, "Thanks for telling me, though."

"I'm sorry. I didn't mean to make it hard on you."

He shrugged and said, "It's okay. Now that the guys know you're Ezekial Tobias, that'll take some of the heat off me. I haven't heard a single 'soft on the inside' remark since last night."

When the rest of the team arrived, Mrs. Gao spoke in a soft tone of voice. "Sundogs, follow me." She pushed open a nearby door then pulled Pow Wow and me into a dimly lit room.

All at once, the lights went on and people started shouting. There were balloons everywhere. A large banner that read "Congratulations!" was hung across the far wall. There was so much excitement, I almost didn't notice the red-haired man propped up in the hospital bed.

Coach Ryan's face was pale, but he was smiling. Mr. Rhea, the Everdine scout, was standing on one side of the coach's bed. Mr. and Mrs. O'Connor were standing on the other side. Coach Ryan started to speak, but it was so noisy in the room that no one could hear him.

Mrs. Gao must have noticed, because she exhaled, "Shhh!"

The room fell quiet.

Coach Ryan's voice was weak, but he seemed determined to speak. "Sundogs, good job out there. Let's hear it for your other coach, Seth Crow." In spite of the I.V. attached to the back of his left hand, the coach started clapping.

Everyone joined in.

Mr. Crow blushed.

When Coach Ryan motioned for us to quiet down, we instantly fell silent.

The coach smiled and said, "Ian Crow, come up here."

Ian walked over to the bed and stood there, looking down. His hair fell down in front of his eyes.

Coach Ryan said, "Ian, I'm sorry to have to tell you…" The coach's voice faded away, and he just shook his head.

Oh, no, I thought. Ian didn't get the scholarship. I felt bad, like there may have been something else I could have done to help him.

The coach took a deep breath and started again. "I'm sorry to have to tell you that, after this tournament, you will no longer play for the Dallas Sundogs."

I glanced over at Pow Wow. From the look on his face, I could tell that he was as confused as me.

Coach Ryan slugged Ian on the arm and continued, "You're not going to be playing for the Sundogs because you're going to be playing for Everdine!"

Ian looked over at the coach, then at Mr. Rhea, who was smiling.

Mr. Rhea then spoke. "Ian Crow, it is with great honor that I inform you that you are the recipient of a full scholarship to play soccer at Everdine Preparatory School for

Boys."

Ian looked down again. Even though his hair covered his eyes, I could still see that he was smiling.

We all crowded around Ian to congratulate him. As the room got noisy again, Mr. Rhea called out, "Just a minute! I'm not finished yet."

All at once, everyone stopped talking and we all looked at Mr. Rhea.

He was still smiling. "It is with great pleasure that I offer this scholarship to Ian Crow on behalf of Everdine Prep. Even so, I have a problem."

We all looked around at each other. What did he mean, a problem?

"I'm still left with two half-scholarships unfilled." He shook his head, but the smile never left his face. "Richard Gao, would you come over here?"

For a moment, even I wondered who Richard Gao was. Then Pow Wow headed off in his direction.

Mr. Rhea then looked at me.

At least, I thought he was looking at me. I glanced over my shoulder to see if maybe he'd been looking at someone behind me. Everybody back there was looking at me, too.

Mr. Rhea cleared his throat and said, "I understand we have a celebrity in our midst. Ezekial Tobias Armstrong, would you come here, too?"

My face felt like it was on fire as I passed through the crowd then stood beside Pow Wow. I looked over to see that he was blushing, too. I felt better knowing I wasn't the only one.

Mr. Rhea slapped us both on the back. "It is also with great pleasure that I announce the winners of Everdine's two half-scholarships: Richard Gao and Zeke Armstrong!"

To be offered a scholarship to Everdine was a great honor, something I never expected, but I wasn't sure if I wanted to leave my uncle and Dallas. No sooner had I thought that, my mobile phone began to ring. It was Uncle Dane. His flight from Paris had just landed in Dallas. He would be in Houston in time for the final game. Uncle Dane said we'd discuss Everdine once we were back in Dallas.

A few minutes after I finished talking to my uncle, Dr. Gao tapped me on the shoulder and said I had a visitor out in the hall. I walked outside to see Detective García standing there. She was holding a large shopping bag in her left hand.

She extended her right hand and, as I shook it, she said, "Zeke, I owe you an apology."

I told her it was okay, that it had all worked out in the end.

"Yes," she replied. "Even so, by not taking you seriously, I jeopardized your life, not to mention Ryan O'Connor's, Luke Whitehead's, and your friends'."

I didn't really know what to say, so I just stood there looking down at the floor.

Detective García reached into the shopping bag and pulled out a book. She held out a pen and a copy of *Ezekial Tobias and the Lost Inca Gold*. "Would you autograph this for me?"

My cheeks got really hot as I signed my name – my full name – on the title page. I told her that if she wanted Uncle Dane to sign it, too, all she'd have to do would be to show up at the Sundogs' championship game.

As I turned to walk back into Coach Ryan's room, Detective García said, "Oh, Zeke. Just a minute…"

I looked back to see her holding two clear plastic bags containing my fake knife and the packets of stage blood.

She handed them to me and said, "I believe these are

yours." The detective gave me a quick wink, then she turned and walked down the corridor.

I thought about rigging up the knife and blood to make it look like I'd been stabbed in the neck. That had been my plan when I found Coach Ryan beside the fence. If I were to walk into the coach's room like that, some of the team moms would gasp out loud, and a lot of the guys would think it was funny. It would have been a good prank, but the next time trouble found me, I wanted people to take me seriously. I threw the fake knife and blood into the trash on my way back into Coach Ryan's room.

Green Streak

Zeke Armstrong goes to New York City for the Big Apple Inline Skate-Off...and takes a bite out of crime. After a skater dressed in green injures an elderly lady in Central Park, the police treat the case as a mugging. Zeke knows it's more than that. He follows the skater to his secret lair and overhears him making mysterious plans with another man to do the lady further harm. Will Zeke figure out what they're up to in time to save the day and skate the final race? Or will the bad guys stop him in his tracks?